WAYNE STINNETT

RISING
STORM

A JESSE MCDERMITT NOVEL

❖ ◆ ❖

Caribbean Adventure Series
Volume 11

DOWN ISLAND PRESS

2017

Published by DOWN ISLAND PRESS, 2017
Lady's Island, SC

Library of Congress cataloging-in-publication Data
Stinnett, Wayne
Rising Storm/Wayne Stinnett
p. cm. - (A Jesse McDermitt novel)
ISBN-10: 0-9981285-5-4
ISBN-13: 978-0-9981285-5-9
Down Island Press, LLC

Graphics by Wicked Good Book Covers
Edited by Larks & Katydids
Final Proofreading by Donna Rich
Interior Design by Write Dream Repeat Book Design

This is a work of fiction. Names, characters, and incidents are either the product of the author's imagination or are used fictitiously. Any resemblance to actual persons, living or dead, businesses, companies, events, or locales is entirely coincidental. Most of the locations herein are also fictional, or are used fictitiously. However, I take great pains to depict the location and description of the many well-known islands, locales, beaches, reefs, bars, and restaurants throughout the Florida Keys and the Caribbean, to the best of my ability.

CHAPTER
ONE

The sun was hot, even though it was a fairly cool day. All around me, glaring white sand bars punctuated the shallow, gin-clear water, and the cobalt sky hung above it. The yellow sand lay just inches below the water's surface, and the bleached white sand rose only inches above it; together they created a swirl of yellow and white, like some sort of salty Rorschach image.

Things had quieted to a level befitting the latitude in the last few weeks, as things here tend to do. Excitement levels are kinda like the weather. If you don't like it, just wait a little while and it'll change. Normally we see long periods of calm before the next storm.

Same with the weather.

The closer you get to the equator—what we call the little latitudes—the more laid-back the lifestyle. We don't worry about heavy coats, galoshes, gloves, snow tires, furnaces, or the like. I guess that leaves us with more time to ponder the important intricacies of life.

Bad things happen anywhere and everywhere; no place is immune anymore, not even paradise. But bad things seldom happen to most people, and between those sorry events there are days, weeks, and months of relative boredom.

I've never been one to get bored. As a kid, if I said I was bored, Dad—or more likely Mom—would quickly find something for me to do to alleviate the boredom.

What many call boredom, I call tranquility.

Friends have asked me on occasion how I can sit for hours contemplating nothing more than the scudding clouds over the shallow flats before a squall. Or just watch the setting sun transform the day to night, for the sheer pleasure of the colors it creates in the sky.

I often find myself mesmerized by the day-to-day life in the shallows of the back-country. These are the things I live for. I've seen enough violence and mayhem to last a few lifetimes.

Sometimes, I let my mind drift—just let it wander around the Glades, Shark River, or Ten Thousand Islands, the area where I grew up. Then I'll let it drift back in time and meander south, down to the Keys. I can see this area the way it must have looked hundreds of years ago, before it was *discovered*—drained, divided, and destroyed. Back to a time when the only humans to see this part of the world were the tribes of people that lived along the southwest coast of Florida, before the Spanish arrived.

The typical tidal pool explorer doesn't often witness any momentous life-changing events—at least not in his own tidal pool. Watching a couple of hermit crabs duking it out over a vacant conch shell, I thought it might be possible that the outcome could mean life or death for one of the

know your way around the maze of unmarked channels, the only way to get to my island is to come down Harbor Channel. It's a natural waterway that opens into the Gulf and runs nearly straight for about three miles to my island, where it turns south and disappears into a network of cuts and passes in the shallows of the back-country. I always know when I have visitors, long before they can even see my house.

Finn's a strong swimmer with great stamina, and I don't have to hold back very much. Over a long swim, like I do every other day to stay in shape, he would need to stop to rest at least once. He's also easily distracted, being at that age where labs are still puppies at heart, but physically full grown. So, on my exercise swims, he stays home.

But since this was Saturday, this was just a fun swim; we stopped several times along the way to explore. Finn has a passion for play. Splash water at him and he tries to catch the biggest drops in his mouth. Another passion is clams. He enjoys diving down to dig them up in the shallows. There aren't a lot of clams in the Keys, but the Contents are more a part of the Gulf of Mexico than the archipelago.

He soon found some, though I had no idea how, so I stopped and waded to the sandbar to survey our surroundings. Sitting on the sand, I could see the deep, blue-gray water of the channel clearly. It stood out in sharp contrast to the sandy yellow bottom of the flats and the blinding white sand bars exposed by the low tide. To the southeast, where the channel turned and disappeared, I could barely make out the low pier that jutted out from my island. On the highest tides, it was only a few inches above the water and nearly invisible at a distance. My house was shielded from view by the taller mangroves and buttonwoods, mostly impenetrable, that surrounded it on three sides.

Finn was laying on the sand, opening and consuming his collection of tasty snacks. He stopped, lifted his head, and stared off to the south, ears and head cocked quizzically.

I'd learned to trust his hearing better than my own, and looked out over the flats in the same direction. "You hear something down that way?"

Whining softly, Finn left his last clam uneaten on the sand bar and trotted to where I sat. Standing, I could hear it too. An outboard engine was moving slowly up through the confusion of narrow channels, working toward us. Higher than idle speed, so it was either someone who knew their way or someone about to run aground.

"We'd best get back to the house," I said to Finn, as I started walking toward the water.

He followed and we began swimming again, angling toward the nearer south pier instead of the floating pier on the north side of the island. Soon we swam across the small channel I'd dredged to the house, and I waited by the ladder at the end of the pier. Finn hadn't quite figured out the ladder—he needed a little help with it still—but there was a small ramp on the north pier that he used to come and go with ease.

The approaching boat was getting closer, but still hadn't reached the deeper water of Harbor Channel, this side of Howe Key. We didn't get many visitors on the island, and I knew the engine sound of those that came out regularly. This wasn't one of them.

Hearing footsteps, I turned around and saw Carl coming down the steps from my deck. Carl Trent and his wife Charlie, along with their two kids, lived on the island and

"Does your friend live here in the Keys?" I asked.

"Her name's Amy. Amy Huggins. They were building a house on No Name Key before her husband Dan was killed. She's still trying to work on it, but she's nearly out of money. She stays in a little trailer on the property."

"What was stolen?"

"She's not really certain," Denise said. "She's not even a hundred percent sure there was anything to be stolen in the first place."

"Wait," I said. "She's not sure if anything was stolen, but wants help in finding it? What is it she thinks *might* have been stolen?"

"She told me she found something—something hidden in a place that should have held a lot more."

Intrigued, but a bit impatient, I asked, "A lot more what, Denise?"

"She found an emerald."

completely off the grid. Electricity comes from generators, or a combination of solar and wind power. Most of the homes are in the center of the north side of the island, with a smaller subdivision at the northeast corner, just north of the abandoned No Name Lodge and the old ferry station. I found the Huggins homestead easily enough, halfway down the first dirt track to the north, off the main road and isolated.

I called out the woman's name as Finn and I walked up a long driveway toward a house under construction. A small trailer—not really a mobile home, but more like a large camper—was parked beside the house.

A noise from the house stopped both of us in our tracks. The sound of a pump shotgun loading a shell is very distinct.

"Who are you and what do you want?" a voice shouted from somewhere inside.

"My name's Jesse," I called back. "Jesse McDermitt. Denise Montrose sent me."

A woman stepped out of the shadowy interior of the elevated cinder block structure. She carried the shotgun in the crook of her right arm, the barrel pointed down at the ground. It was obvious from the casual way she carried it that she was familiar with the weapon.

"Denise called me an hour ago," she said. "I'm Amy Huggins."

Finn and I waited where we stood, as Amy walked down the steps toward us. A woman with a shotgun is always in charge.

At first glance, she didn't look to be several years older, as Denise had said. Aside from the ripeness of her belly, she looked very fit and healthy, with dark tanned skin wherever it was exposed—which wasn't much. She wore denim pants, and a long-sleeved work shirt to protect her from the sun. A faded ball cap sat slightly crooked on her head, and wild, dark-brown hair hung from the back of the cap, past her shoulders. Several loose strands of hair fell on either side, framing a very pretty face.

"You don't look like what I expected," she said, stopping in front of me. Finn angled himself between us, and she reached down and let him sniff her hand for a second, then casually scratched the spot behind his ear. "I somehow pictured you in a gray suit, with a hat."

"I'm not a TV private eye," I said. "Just a guy who fishes and owns part of a security business."

"Denise didn't mention that," Amy said. "Want to go inside and get out of the heat?"

"The heat doesn't bother me," I said. "But it might be a good idea in your case."

"Because I'm pregnant? I was born on a boat, Mister McDermitt. And my son will be born in this house, if I can get it finished in time."

Finn and I followed her—not to the trailer, but toward the house.

"You're building this yourself?" I asked.

"Pretty much," she replied matter-of-factly, as if every pregnant woman was a construction worker. "Every block laid and every nail driven was done by either myself or my late husband before he was killed. Lately, I've had to hire help here and there."

She walked through the unfinished doorway into a central room with a low, vaulted ceiling. The unfinished floor felt solid, and there were no creaks—a testament to good workmanship. A table with two folding chairs stood

They weren't on the plans, and Dan said he just decided to add them."

"I see," I said, squatting beside the remnants of the post and looking at the broken blocks. It was obvious they'd been removed without finesse, smashed with a sledgehammer. Rising, I stepped over to the other post and slapped my palm on the capstone. It sounded solid. "Got a hammer?"

Amy disappeared inside and returned a moment later with a big framing hammer.

I took it and tapped lightly on the capstone, so as not to leave a mark. "This one's poured solid."

"Everything is," she said. "Dan sunk two dozen well points around the perimeter before digging the footers, and pumped water out for two days before pouring. Concrete extends four feet below grade, poured on top of ancient limestone and coral. Every course was poured solid, with half-inch steel reinforcement rods all the way up to the rafters."

"Hurricane proof," I said, looking at the broken post again.

"Wind- and wave-proof at least."

I nodded. "Nothing stops a tidal surge."

"We're higher than the record storm surge of thirty-five, and the first floor is the garage and Dan's man-cave."

"Obviously, your husband hid something of value inside this post. Just from what I've seen, he wasn't the kind of man to cut the corners off blocks, just to save a buck. And if it were just the single stone, the cavity is overkill."

"It was more than just the one emerald," Amy said. "Whatever was in there, Wilson Carmichael took."

"Was anything else missing when you returned?"

"Nothing at all," she replied. "And like I said, he left behind everything he'd arrived here with, plus a week's pay."

"And you have no idea where he went?"

"If I did, Mister McDermitt, I'd have gone and got back what rightfully belongs to my boy."

I looked up at her. She stood on the porch, feet firmly planted, hands on her hips. She was a little taller than most women, probably close to five-nine. It looked like she was nearly full term, and probably weighed over one-seventy. The extra weight of the baby didn't seem to slow her in any way. I imagine she was every bit as tough as she sounded, and the look on her face was one of total resolve. Someone had taken something from this woman. How her husband came across it and why he hid it in the post didn't matter to her. Right or wrong, her husband was dead and she had a son to raise.

I mounted the steps and stood in front of her on the porch, studying her face. "What did your husband do in the Army?"

She turned and went back inside the house. I followed her and we sat at the table again. I noticed a note pad with two columns of numbers scrawled across the top page. There were notes next to each number in the second column—a materials list. The other column had no notes, but the sum at the bottom was less than the sum of the materials list. An income list? If so, Amy Huggins was sinking all she had into the house and wouldn't have enough to finish.

"Dan was an engineer," she said. "He was in South America to survey several possible locations for a new Army base."

CHAPTER
THREE

Shadows were stretching across the canal ahead as I piloted the Grady into the channel toward the *Rusty Anchor*. I slowed and entered the canal, looking longingly at my plane, *Island Hopper*. Her red skin practically glowed in the dappled sunlight coming through the mangroves across the canal. Maybe Devon would agree to go flying tomorrow.

I tied off in front of the *Rusty Tiki*, a floating bar Rusty had built on a skiff's hull. He'd hired a guy to operate the only floating Tiki bar taxi in the Middle Keys, and it seemed to be working pretty well.

Finn ran to his favorite gumbo-limbo tree and hiked his leg on it. Then he took off around the corner of the bar toward the deck and the large, open yard beyond.

There weren't many cars in the lot, and when I entered there were only a few men at a table by a window. They each looked up and nodded. I nodded back, then went to the bar and took my usual seat. I didn't know the men personally, but recognized them as locals.

Leaning over the bar, I opened the cooler and felt around until I found the familiar stubby bottle. Rusty came out of the office, talking to Sam Romano, his new Tiki taxi driver. I used one of the openers laying on the bar to pop the top on my first beer of the day.

"Hey, Sam," I said, tipping my bottle toward the man. He was bald, mostly by choice. Having a receding hairline, he'd opted for the shaved look, resulting in a well-tanned skull. He sported a small, neatly trimmed goatee.

"Hi, Jesse," Sam replied. "How've you been?"

"Never mind how he's been." Rusty handed Sam a case full of liquor bottles from behind the bar. "He don't never change. Those fellas at the table need a lift out to Carlton's yacht in the harbor. He's having a party and folks will be coming and going from *Dockside* all evening."

"All this for Mister Carlton?"

"Yeah," Rusty said, walking him around the bar. "He's gonna pay you in cash, four hundred. Plus another four to run folks back and forth. Bring me back six bills and you keep the rest, plus any tips. Okay?"

Sam grinned and nodded, then greeted the men at the table, telling them they could board at any time. Rusty had told me that Sam was making at least a hundred a night in tips, so he was gonna have a good day today.

"I got her going again," Rusty said, returning to his place behind the bar. Rather than buy a new motor for his skiff, he'd been working on the old one for two weeks.

He was picking up a conversation that we'd started days ago, when I came down to pick up some new reels I'd ordered. That's the way things are in the Keys. You might

turned west in a wide circle. The *Rusty Tiki* was just turning into Sister Creek.

"That's the oddest boat I've ever seen," Devon said, eyeing the former flats skiff with part of Rusty's deck on top of it.

"It definitely draws attention," I said. "People ride on it, just for the novelty. He charges five bucks from any one stop to another, or ten for a two-hour ride from bar to bar."

Devon shouted over the wind. "The sun's going down."

I pushed the throttle to the stop as I lined up on the center span of the Seven Mile Bridge. The little boat surged forward to top speed, riding smoothly on the glassy water.

"We'll get there in time," I shouted back.

Devon leaned against me, still holding the T-top rail. I put my arm around her, pulling her in closer. In the turbulent air behind the console and windscreen, I caught an occasional whiff of her shampoo—a sort of tropical flower scent that I couldn't put my finger on, but it smelled good.

True to my word, we arrived back at the island with the sun still a few degrees above the western horizon. "Just drop your bag in the house," I said, tying off. "Grab a bottle and a couple of glasses, and I'll be out there in a few minutes."

Devon opened the door for Finn and they went up to the deck together while I raised the outboard. I quickly hooked the freshwater washdown hose to the muffs and placed them over the intakes on the lower unit. Turning the water on, I started the engine and let it run for a couple of minutes, then shut it off and turned off the water.

When I got up to the deck, I quickly looked inside. Devon's bag was just inside the door, so I continued to the back steps, where I found her jacket, laying across the railing. She and Finn were out at the end of the north pier and I sat down next to her. I noticed she wasn't wearing her shoulder holster. "Where's your gun?"

"I stuck it in my bag," she replied, leaning against me. "I can't be a cop all the time."

I'd met Devon when she was working a serial killer case. The psycho killed Denise's dad, Kevin Montrose, after killing three others. A friend had been wrongly accused of the first two murders—Jim Isaksson and his diver, Jenny Marshall. Fortunately, he'd been in custody when a topless dancer on Stock Island was murdered.

Since then, Devon and I had been together for whatever free time she could get away from her job as a Monroe County Sheriff's detective. Sometimes here on the island, sometimes her place in Key West, and occasionally a little bed and breakfast up-island.

As we shared the wine, the sun slowly got closer and closer to the horizon. There were no clouds to the west and just a few scattered clouds overhead. They began to change to a burnt orange as a breeze kicked up out of the east, chasing the sun. The air carried the scent of frangipani and jasmine, sea salt, the iodine smell of the back-country, and a mixture of other exotic scents.

Sol quietly slipped below the horizon, and when the last of the red-orange orb was about to disappear I saw Devon close her eyes to make a wish. The sun vanished uneventfully over the far horizon, and it grew dark quickly. Stars began to take the place of the sunlight and the moon seemed to grow brighter, as our eyes adjusted to the fading light.

"It's never boring out here," Devon said, rubbing the inside of my leg.

pool, knowing that won't happen out here. But we don't *have* to go to sleep right away, do we?"

We woke a little after sunrise. Devon went to the guest cabin, where she'd left her bag. Storage space on a boat is at a premium, and only half the drawers in the guest cabin were empty. In the galley, I loaded a cooler with bottles of water and bowls of sliced fruit. Devon came up the steps wearing a little green bikini top and a pair of worn, cut-off jeans, the top button unfastened. Her skin was nearly as tan as my own. Looked a lot better, though.

"How far is this tidal pool?" she asked, opening one of the containers and putting a chunk of mango in her mouth.

"Not far. Less than a mile."

We stepped out of the cabin into the humid air trapped below the house.

Devon looked around. "Which boat are we taking?"

"We're not taking a boat," I said, leading her out the door and up the steps. Finn bounded ahead of us.

"We're walking?"

"It's too shallow for a boat," I replied. "Don't worry, you'll barely get your knees wet."

With Finn's help, we found the little tidal pool again. The exposed sand flat that encircled it was so low that it wasn't even visible from just a hundred yards away.

I spread a large blanket on the bright white sand. "We only have a few hours before this will be under water."

"I don't get it," she said. "There's nothing here."

"Take your shorts off and wade out into the pool. It's been landlocked for hours and a lot of the water has evaporated."

Devon wiggled her hips as her shorts came down, and she dropped them on the blanket. "Are you joining me?"

"Yeah," I replied, as I walked with her to the edge of the small tidal pool, "but I want to see your reaction."

"Reaction to what?" She took a tentative step into the clear water.

"Just indulge me," I said, with a grin and a wink.

She waded into the water, which quickly rose to waist-deep. I wasn't worried that it would be cold. Even in the winter, the water doesn't get very cold here; tidal pools, being separated from the surrounding water, warmed quickly.

"The water's a lot hotter than what we waded through to get here," Devon said, turning and facing me. "Is that it?"

"Part of it," I responded, taking a few steps into the warm water. "Lay back and float."

"I don't float," she said, putting her hands on her hips. "You know that."

"Amuse me. This water's a little different."

Slowly, Devon lowered herself into the warm water. When the water reached her shoulders, her legs nearly slipped out from under her, and she floated easily, like a cork.

"What the hell?" she exclaimed, twisting her body to get her feet back under her, and standing up.

"Most of the water's evaporated," I said, walking out toward her. "The salinity in this pool is twice that of the water around it, I bet. No chance of even a non-swimmer sinking in water like this."

described the boat, and the work that was going to be done. Deuce said he'd have Tony call as soon as he found out something.

Ending the call, I turned back to Rusty. "You think this King Buck will be around this evening?"

"Not right away," Rusty said. "I haven't talked to him. He's keeping a low profile. But I talked to Ray Floyd, at the airport. He said that Buck took his plane up this morning with a couple of fishermen. Probably won't be back until dark."

"I'll wait until morning," I said. "Give me an excuse to get in the air after my swim."

I finished my beer, said goodbye to Rusty, and slapped my thigh as I headed toward the door. Finn rose from his spot in the corner and trotted along beside me back down to the Grady.

She stopped and looked deep into my eyes. Finally, she said, "My boat's somewhere in the Virgin Islands. The boat I came here on is anchored beyond the three-mile limit, north of Bluefish Bank."

I glanced off to the northeast, though I knew Bluefish was a good fifteen miles away, far beyond line of sight. "You rowed all that way?"

"Motored the first five miles," she replied, as we reached the tiny beach. "I rowed the rest since about midnight."

"You must be worn out," I said. I took her hand and led her toward the base of the fallen coconut palm. "Come with me. I have something for you."

Dropping to my knees, I quickly excavated the spot where I'd buried the box. "I didn't know when or even if you'd get here, so I put this out here several days ago."

"What is it?" she asked, as I lifted the watertight box from the hole.

I looked up at her. Physically, she hadn't changed a bit in the year and a half since I'd last seen her. If anything, she was more fit and tanned than ever. But there was something to her eyes—some emptiness, like you see in old folks who are just counting the days until they die.

"I don't know your situation," I replied, opening the box. "Stockwell told us a little about what you were doing, after I figured out what was going on. All I know about the present is that he ordered you home, since the whole team is being deactivated. I read your reply and gathered that you don't trust him for whatever reason." Removing a carton from the watertight box, I handed it to her. "This is a sat-phone, brand new, never used. I turned it on once and saved the number of a second one I bought at the same time and will keep for myself. If you feel the need, you can call me anytime. Neither has ever been turned on anywhere near my regular phone, or any other phones for that matter."

She took the carton and stared down at me. "Jim Franklin's little black box?"

Franklin is a retired spook that worked with Deuce on occasion. He's also an electronics tech and one of the best surveillance guys in the business. He invented a machine that would scan a given cellphone's location and track any other phones in its vicinity. Over time, it would report multiple close geographic contacts between the target phone and any other. His thinking was that bad guys usually associate with other bad guys, and whenever the bad guy in question was with another person more than once, they were probably meeting; he could then track two bad guys' phones.

"Yeah," I replied. "Don't turn it on anywhere around here, though. If you're that worried, I mean."

"Do I have reason to worry?" she asked. "And what's this about the team being dissolved?"

"I'll let you figure out the answer to the first question. Ask me anything you want, and if I know, I'll tell you. You can decide for yourself about whether you should worry about anything."

"And the team?"

"There's an election next month," I replied. "Stockwell says that no matter who the next president is, the team will be pretty much broken up immediately, and everyone sent back to their parent commands. He's gone above and beyond to make sure everyone lands on their feet, even arranging early retirement for Deuce and a couple

From the high vantage point of the deck, I could see Charity on the pier, rinsing the seawater from her hair. The same warm water from the cistern above me was cascading down her nude body. A splash of color on the pier railing showed where she'd left her bikini.

My face flushed, and I quickly looked away and turned off the water. No doubt she was an attractive woman—many would say drop-dead gorgeous—but I'd never seen her in that way. She was a friend, and a former co-worker.

And, frankly, not altogether right in the head, making her easily manipulated. Plus she was quite a few years younger than me.

Devon is younger, too, the pervert on my shoulder reminded me as I went inside to change.

After getting into a clean pair of jeans, a long-sleeved work shirt, and nearly worn-out boat shoes, I pulled open a drawer and took out a holstered nine-millimeter Sig-Sauer P226, clipping it inside the waistband of my pants behind my back.

I almost collided with Charity when I pulled the door open and stepped out onto the deck.

"Are you sure nobody will know me where we're going?" she asked, stepping back.

"Rusty will," I said, just a bit flustered. I was having a hard time getting the image of her naked body out of my mind.

"The fat, bald guy?" she asked. "He's your friend, right?"

"Yeah," I said, putting on my sunglasses and trying to regain my composure. "I can't pull into the *Anchor* and not stop in. But one word from me and he'll be the only one to know. Don't let his girth fool you; he can still move pretty quickly. *That* man, I trust one hundred percent."

After telling Finn to stay, I took the little Grady again. Not knowing what the weather would be in the afternoon, I preferred its solid ride in a chop a lot more than my Maverick, or the runabout Carl and I had built. Finn had only been up in the plane with me once and he didn't seem to care for it.

Charity and I didn't talk much as I brought the Grady up on plane in Harbor Channel. She seemed to relax against the leaning post next to me as we made a wide turn south, following about three feet of water through the shallows. Straightening on a course that would take us to the Seven Mile Bridge, which was just out of sight, I glanced over at her.

She seemed very calm and was smiling. She wore khaki shorts and a loose-fitting, navy-blue pullover blouse with a wide neckline hanging over a bare shoulder. She moved easily with the boat, reading the waves and shifting her body, without having to hang onto the T-top rail. Our shoulders or hips occasionally bumped, reminding me of the proximity.

"Are you carrying?" I asked, raising my voice against the buffeting wind.

"Everywhere I go," she replied, looking out over the water. "You?"

"Most of the time," I replied, looking forward again.

"Who are you going to see in Key West?"

"Friend of a friend," I said. "He's an archaeologist and might know something about an emerald I have."

"An emerald?"

I reached into my pocket and pulled the folded handkerchief out, letting it fall open behind the windscreen, as I held the stone firmly. I opened my hand slightly, to keep the wind from yanking the handkerchief out of my hand.

blade and fired. It coughed once, belching a cloud of thick blue-gray smoke, and then it settled into its typical rumbling idle.

I signaled Mac with my thumb and he quickly released the tie-downs, then climbed into the right-hand seat and buckled in. He started to yell over the engine noise, but I pointed to a set of headphones hanging in front of him.

While the engine warmed up, I called Miami Center to check air traffic and inform them of our intent. Then I gave Mac a quick briefing of the radio and GPS, before releasing the brakes and taxiing down toward the boat ramp. A Beaver on land is an awkward and ungainly beast, bouncing with every crack in the concrete. With the wings and cabin roof nearly ten feet above the ground, the bouncing caused violent swaying in the cockpit, so we went very slowly.

As we reached the end of the ramp, the bouncing gave way to the smooth feel of the water, as the pontoons lifted the wheels from the bottom. Moving the landing gear lever to the retracted position, I lowered the rudders and waited for the four blue lights to come on to show that all four wheels had retracted into the pontoons and were locked.

The pontoons knifed through the light chop as I steered the plane into the channel running southeast out of Rusty's canal. The crab trap floats that lined the edges of the channel made a perfect runway into the southeast wind.

Raising the rudders, I advanced the throttle. The engine roared as the *Hopper* picked up speed. The old bird responded instantly; within seconds we were skimming across Vaca Key Bight. It only took a few hundred yards before I felt the pontoons lift out of the water, and then we were airborne. The right pontoon caught a wave and lifted slower than the other, as sometimes happens in water that's not perfectly calm. The drag on that pontoon fishtailed the plane slightly as we soared into the sky. I kicked the rudder pedal, and *Island Hopper* responded quickly, straightening out.

I banked right and made a long sweeping turn to starboard, away from Key Colony Beach. I leveled off at fifteen hundred feet and called on the common traffic advisory frequency that we were clear to the south. Pointing the nose slightly south of west, I started following the Overseas Highway toward the end of the road.

As we flew along the Seven Mile Bridge, Mac seemed to be studying the horizon ahead. I had no idea where exactly he wanted to go, but I figured it wouldn't be boring.

"Key West up there," I said, reaching for the mic. I radioed who I was, our position, and intent to Key West air traffic control. "Just letting them know who we are," I told my passengers, trying to lighten the mood. Charity still hadn't spoken to Mac. "Don't need any company from the boys at Truman."

Mac nodded, and seemed to be searching the horizon beyond Key West.

"If you've got numbers," I said, pointing to one of the few instruments in the plane I knew Mac would be familiar with, "enter them in the GPS and we'll do a flyover."

Pulling a wrinkled piece of paper from his pocket, Mac entered the coordinates into the unit and hit the *Go* button. A quick glance told me we were only a few degrees off course and I made an adjustment.

"You want them to see us or not?" I asked, getting the feeling that this was more than just a missing homing device.

I did remember that Stockwell had told me it was an antique sailing yacht. "What's she like?"

"Her name's *Wind Dancer*," Charity replied, an almost wistful look on her face. She went on to tell me all about her boat, how it looked, how it handled, and how it made her feel. Obviously, it would be hard for her to part with it—something I completely understood.

"I can buy it," she said, at last. "At least, I think I can. That is, if everything is going away, like you said."

"Even Travis's job is going away," I said. "Look, you know all the electronic gadgets that Chyrel worked with? The computers, bugs, trackers, hidden cameras, and stuff? Travis gave it all to Deuce. Just up and handed it all over, said it was never listed as government property. Probably a hundred-grand worth of equipment. I wouldn't be surprised if the same is true for your boat."

"Is there any way you could find out?" she asked. "Without raising any suspicions?"

"Maybe. But I know someone who can find out for sure. It just depends on how much you trust her."

"Chyrel?"

I nodded.

She thought about it a moment. "Yeah, I trust her," she finally said.

"I'll contact her," I said. "We have a back-channel way, kinda like that sat-phone I gave you."

The sound of a radial engine is very distinctive and I had no doubt that if there were any pilots on the island and they heard it, they'd be searching the sky for us. I hoped our little extracurricular excursion hadn't caused us to miss Buck Reilly.

"It was mined by slaves long before then, in what is now Ecuador. Aztec raids extended all the way into South America at one time. If I were to guess, it was probably mined in the thirteenth or early fourteenth century."

"You can tell all that, just by looking at it?" Charity asked.

"Its origins are obvious," Reilly said. "The inclusions, color, and hue are clearly indicative of emeralds mined in Ecuador. As to the specific stone, I've studied the lost treasure of Cortes for years. I know every rock, coin, ingot, and bar that was recorded on the manifest. That's one of them. No doubt in my mind."

"Lost treasure?" I asked.

"First contact with Europeans, 1519," Reilly began, sounding like a college professor, though he didn't look to be more than thirty years old. "Just twenty-seven years after Columbus. The Aztec ruler at the time was Montezuma. Cortes landed with an armada of ships, and legend has it that, as a peace offering, Montezuma gave Cortes a huge emerald that was said to have mystical powers that could divine truth. It came to be known as *Isabella's Emerald.* Along with this giant emerald, he supposedly gave Cortes two chests of smaller, though still quite large, raw emeralds as a gift to King Charles the Fifth of Spain."

"Cortes accepted it, or so the legend goes. Most likely he just took it. We found a document in the General Archive of the Indies in Seville, Spain that said upon his return, Cortes offered the giant stone to Queen Isabella in the hope that she could convince Charles to fund further conquests in the new world. He really wanted to be appointed the governor of New Spain. The Spanish coffers were nearly empty after wars with England and France, so Charles was forced to decline. Instead, Cortes gave the emerald to his bride, in exchange for a dowry that would fund his next expedition."

Reilly flipped a page in his folder, which was thick with plastic archival sleeves, and he ran his finger down some text while he read. Then he looked up.

"Some two-hundred-and-forty years later, in 1757, Cortes's descendants were extremely wealthy, having conquered most of Central and South America. They'd milked the land and its people dry of anything valuable by then, but they wanted more land grants from Spain. King Ferdinand the Sixth sent a courier to Cartagena to negotiate a price. He carried the signet ring of Cortes as identification. Once the deal was struck, he was to escort a treasure back to Spain, the likes of which would boggle the mind. The treasure included the mystical *Isabella's Emerald*, said to be over nine hundred carats—the same one that was given to Cortes by Montezuma himself. The deal also included two chests full of cut and polished emeralds, plus gold and jade death masks of the Aztec Emperors, several mysterious crystal skulls, gold idols, and various instruments of human sacrifice. This was to be a gift to Ferdinand, in exchange for the land grants." He paused. "Unfortunately, the ship and its treasures were lost at sea."

"And this?" I said, holding up the green stone. "You think it was one of the smaller emeralds in one of those chests?"

"Absolutely no doubt in my mind, whatsoever. It's one of the lost Cortes emeralds."

"So, how was this stone found?" I asked, enthralled by the story of ancient treasure. Rusty had told me the man had a reputation as a world-renowned archeologist and treasure hunter, and Buck Reilly didn't disappoint.

"The ship went down in the Bermuda Triangle," Reilly continued. "Another ship's captain noted the sinking in his log, saying that the treasure ship was ablaze and sank, giving the distance in time and speed from the last land they'd seen. Nobody knows what caused the fire."

"When was the treasure recovered?" Charity asked.

"In 1992, descendants of Cortes approached Doctor Victor Benilous, a well-known archaeologist and the president of an organization called Archaeological Discovery Ventures. They wanted him to locate the shipwreck. Believe it or not, Benilous brought in psychics to help locate the wreck. Two of them, working independently, gave ADV locations that were nearly on top of each other. Using sonar, they found five wrecks in that location, one being the treasure ship they were after. Fast forward a couple of years, and part of the treasure disappeared from a display at the *Museo Nacional de Antropología* in Mexico City. Specifically, one of the small chests of emeralds. The one that held that one. It wasn't the first time the anthropology museum had been robbed."

Reilly snapped his folder of archives closed and watched my eyes.

"Let me get this straight," I said. "That rock was dug up by Montezuma's slaves over five hundred years ago, taken from the Aztecs by the Spaniards, lost at sea, recovered, and was stolen again from this Benilous guy?"

"Word is that the missing chest of emeralds has been bought and sold, or stolen, several times in the last fifteen years. All through the black market, of course, since the stones are pretty easily identifiable. Hence, the lowball price to sell it for you."

"The black market, huh?" I said, looking over at Charity. "That's how you'd turn it fast? What if you went slower and found just the right buyer?"

"Twelve thousand, easy," Reilly said. "But I'm neither in the market, nor do I like the idea of being a go-between."

"What would the whole chest be worth?"

Reilly leaned forward. "You know where the rest are?"

"No, but I think I might know where to look."

He sat back in his seat and scratched at an eyebrow with one finger. "If the chest were available, and it was whole.... There were supposed to be over five hundred emeralds that size in it, I would consider acting as a go-between for ten percent and could turn them into a cool million in less than a week. Two mil, if I sold them one at a time over a period of maybe a year. They're too recognizable to dump on the market individually all at once."

"I'll definitely keep that in mind," I said, folding the stone back into the handkerchief and putting it in my pocket.

"Well, if I can be of any help, let me know," Reilly said, climbing out through the open door, and offering Charity a hand. "But only on the down-low and in person. I'm not exactly popular in the antiquities community these days."

Leaving Buck and his Widgeon, Charity and I started back toward the *Hopper*. "Are you hungry?" I asked.

"Famished," she replied, "but I don't know about going into town. Keeping a low profile has gotten to be a habit."

"There's a restaurant here," I said. "It's passable food and way overpriced, but within walking distance. Or I can call a friend who drives a taxi, and we can go a few blocks to Blue Heaven. This time of day, there won't be but a handful of hungover tourists there for lunch."

She stopped under the starboard wing and looked back toward Reilly's plane.

"What was your first impression of him?" she asked, watching Reilly walking into the Landmark Aviation building.

"A little sketchy, but forthright," I replied. "Something seems to be going on in his life, some big change."

"Yeah, I got that, too. But he gave off an honest vibe."

"Lunch?"

"Okay, but not the overpriced place. And just to be on the safe side, call me Gabby Fleming."

As we retraced our steps, I fished my phone out of my pocket, and pulled up Lawrence Lovett's phone number. He was an old friend who owned his own taxi and had helped me out with good information in the past.

He answered immediately. "Cap'n Jesse! How yuh been, mon?"

We talked for a moment, as Charity and I walked toward the building. "I'm here on the Rock," I said. "At the airport. Can you come and pick me up?"

"Better dan dat," he replied. "I'm already here. Just come to di taxi stand out front. I wait for you."

I ended the call and we hurried through the terminal. There were two taxis ahead of Lawrence's big Crown Victoria, and each driver in turn asked if we needed a ride.

Lawrence saw us approaching and, seeing that I wasn't alone, he hurried around to the passenger side to open the back door.

"Blue Heaven," I told him. "And take the scenic route."

"Yes, suh," the old Androsian replied.

He drove out of the airport and turned left, in the opposite direction from the restaurant. Within minutes, he'd turned left and right so many times through residential areas that I wasn't even sure where we were. Charity kept glancing back through the back window.

We finally turned onto Thomas Street and pulled over to the curb, just past Petronia Street. I handed Lawrence a twenty over the seat and asked him to pick us up in thirty minutes.

Instead of going inside, I led Charity to the left, through the gate and into the backyard. As predicted, there was just a single couple occupying a table. Well, the couple did have company, in the form of several chickens pecking at the ground all around the yard, but that's normal in Key Weird.

We took a table in the corner and both sat with our backs to the wooden fence.

"This is where Tina worked, isn't it?" Charity asked, after memorizing the faces of the young tourist couple.

I'd dated Tina LaMons briefly a few years ago. She and Charity were friends, going back to when both women had been on the Olympic swim team.

"Yeah," I replied. And changing the subject, I added, "Another friend used to be the chef here. She's moved on, but the food's still good."

A waitress came and took our orders. When she'd left, Charity said, "What is it you're working on? The emerald, I mean."

"I'm not sure if I want anyone to know yet. A friend of a friend had something stolen—or, to be exact, her late husband had something stolen. I said I'd look into it, but until I'm sure that the late husband didn't steal it in the first place, I don't want to involve anyone else."

"Jesse, you're talking about ethics with someone who has been a government assassin for over a year."

"Keyword: government," I replied, looking her straight in the eye. "Would you help a thief get back something another thief stole?"

"Depends on who I'm doing it for," she said without hesitation.

"Okay, I see your point. And from my side, it's a very valid point. The widow is pregnant and nearly broke, her late husband was a soldier. If it turns out that the dead soldier was also a thief, I may still get back what was stolen for her. If what Reilly said is to be believed, there'd be no way to return it to its proper owner."

"So, you think there was more than just the one emerald? The whole chest?"

"I think so," I replied.

Charity looked across the yard, at the people walking past on the sidewalk. "A lot of places I've been the last few years, the ethical and moral lines become very blurred."

"Not from where I stand," I replied. "Right is right and wrong is wrong. I stay on this side of where I *know* the line is. But if staying on this side means innocent people might get hurt, I have no trouble crossing that line and taking the fight to the wrong-doers on their own terms."

"So, this lady's pregnant and needs help. I'm guessing the police are out." She studied my face a moment. The two of us had shared some dark secrets in the past and knew things about one another that nobody else knew. I nodded and she continued. "You know you're going to help her, right or wrong. so just get on with it. You helped me more than you will ever know. I owe my life to you and the things I learned from you. Let me help."

"Stockwell wants to debrief you."

"Let *him* wait," she said, as the waitress came with our meal.

"Jesse?" a familiar voice called out from the gate. "I thought I saw you come in here."

I turned and saw Devon and another detective walking toward us with the hostess. I didn't recognize the man; he was coatless, wearing a short-sleeve white shirt and dark blue tie. His detective shield was prominently displayed on his belt, just in front of the pistol on his hip.

"You're sure it's Carmichael?"

"Yeah," Tony replied. "Mistrall said he had an old salvage boat coming up for a refit. He even mentioned the man's name. If he doesn't show up, I'm supposed to bring Deuce's boat there for some work."

"You used Deuce's boat as part of your cover?"

"Only yacht I'm familiar with," Tony said, backing out of the parking spot, and turning toward the road.

"Can you hang out there and see where Carmichael goes after he drops off the boat?"

"Did you know Deuce bought a brand-new Suburban?" Tony asked.

"Um, no."

"That's what he gave me to drive up here in," Tony said. "A black Suburban."

"Hot and a little conspicuous for surveillance, huh?"

Tony glanced at the dash, where a digital display showed an interior temperature of a hundred-and-twenty degrees. He laughed. "We've both been in hotter places."

"Try to find a shady spot. Somewhere you can see the channel and the front of the store. Let me know when you know something."

"Shade in Miami?" Tony said with a chuckle. "What's this all about, Jesse?"

"Carmichael might have stolen something from a friend of a friend, only she doesn't know what it was and can't go to the police, because of the unknown circumstances surrounding how her late husband came to have it."

"This is gonna be one of those pro bono cases, like you talked about last month?"

"The woman's pregnant and her husband was a soldier."

"Nuff said," Tony quipped, turning onto the street.

"It's looking like the husband stashed a small fortune in Aztec emeralds in the house that he and the wife were building. Carmichael arrived shortly after his death, saying he'd served with the husband and offering to help finish the house. It appears that he found what the husband hid."

"Aztec?" Tony whistled softly. "The husband tell her that's what they were?"

"It doesn't look like she even knew it was there. There's evidence that he hid a small chest in a concrete post at the bottom of the back steps. Carmichael found it and disappeared."

Stopping at the corner, Tony waited for traffic to clear, then turned left. "What makes her think it was a chest of ancient jewels?"

"The thief left one behind. I'm in Key West right now and just had an expert look at it. He says it was mined about seven hundred years ago, in Ecuador."

"Dayum!" Tony exclaimed.

"I'd like to help her if I can. Carmichael left Ramrod yesterday morning. Should be there before dark. Let me know when he arrives."

Ending the call, Tony circled the block looking for a shady spot with a view. After a few minutes, he found the closest thing to shade available: a half-dead willow tree in the parking lot of a strip mall next door to the boat shop. At least a nice breeze was blowing off the water behind the strip mall. He parked with as much of the big SUV under what little shade the tree provided and buzzed all the windows down.

Opening the storage compartment in the console, Tony took out a pair of powerful binoculars and began scanning the water behind the shop. He had a clear view of

"A month? She's serious. Just meeting her, she struck me as the kind of woman who doesn't waste time."

When we got back to the *Hopper*, I noticed that Buck Reilly's plane was gone. Walking around the plane, I found five of the holes, three in the fuselage and two near the starboard wingtip, three entries and two exits. Either a bullet was somewhere in the plane, or it had exited somewhere I couldn't see. Neither made the *Hopper* unsafe.

I got the old bird started, received taxi instructions, and a few minutes later we were back in the air, banking out over the back-country to the northeast.

I flew a straight-line course toward my island. We did a low and slow flyover to check for anything floating in the water. Not seeing anything, I lined up on Harbor Light and brought the *Hopper* down in the skinny water north of the island where Charity's dinghy was hidden. I idled toward the north shore where I knew it was a little deeper, up close to the little island.

"Bring your dinghy over to the north dock," I said, as Charity unbuckled and opened her door.

She nodded, hung her headset on the hook, and stepped out onto the pontoon, the wash from the prop snapping at her clothes. When I reached the shallows close to the island, Charity stepped off and I waited a couple of seconds before pushing the left pedal to move out to deeper water. Though it was only three-quarters of a mile to my dock, idling on the surface was out of the question. I'd have the wind at my tail, where a gust could lift it and dive a pontoon. Quick way to sink your aircraft.

Turning into the wind, I powered up. The *Hopper* did its magical transformation from boat to plane again and

I was quickly in the air. I circled the little island, low and slow, watching Charity pull the palm fronds off the dinghy.

When I saw that she'd pushed it out and climbed in, I banked and flew west past my island. When I banked again for an upwind approach to the shallows north of my island, I could see her little dinghy skipping across the wave tops.

Charity was already on the pier, when I idled up to it, her dinghy pulled up on the sand at the foot of the pier. She ducked easily under the wing as I killed the engine and looped a dock line around the aft cleat of the pontoon. Letting the *Hopper's* momentum slowly drift her up against the fenders, Charity quickly had the bird secured to the pier's T-dock. Unlike the south pier, this one floated. Built on thirty-gallon plastic drums up in Homestead, it was brought out to me in several pieces by barge when I built the bunkhouses.

Finn was waiting on the pier as well, and acted like I'd been gone for months. I didn't leave him alone very often, and though he was physically full-grown he still had the mind of a pup.

"Hi there, Finn," Charity said, squatting down to greet him face-to-face with a double ear scratch.

I suddenly felt kind of self-conscious, remembering her showering naked and realizing we would be the only two here, at least until tomorrow.

"I got him up in South Carolina earlier in the year. We'd better hurry, fifteen miles by dinghy and then another fifteen in a sailboat will take us until almost dark."

Telling Finn to stay ashore once more, we stepped down into the little dinghy. It had a single bench seat at the

I touched the little cog to access the settings, and saw that there were two depth alarms. One was set for ten feet and the other for seven. The second was probably set very near the maximum draft, to warn the captain to stop before running aground, so I assumed it had been zeroed to the surface and the keel was somewhere less than seven feet below. Good to know.

I didn't know what the draft on this boat was, but I was pretty certain it was less than ten feet, and probably six. I knew the water ahead like most people know the streets of their hometown, and there wasn't anything shallower than about fifteen feet between here and Harbor Key.

Charity had been gone several minutes. Finally, she appeared at the hatch, lifting a small cooler up to the cockpit deck ahead of her. She'd changed into a bikini.

"I see you found the nerve center," she said, opening the cooler and taking two bottles out. She opened them both, handing me a bottle of Kofresi.

"Yeah," I replied, taking a long pull from the bottle. "And I see you stopped in Puerto Rico on the way. Old Harbor makes a fine stout."

"Hope you don't mind," she said, stretching out on the long bench. "I like to get some sun at least a few times a week and haven't had much of a chance in a while."

Charity had spent nearly a month aboard the *Revenge* as we went from one port to another, searching for Jason Smith all over the western Caribbean. We'd shared a lot of words, slowly opening up to each other. In the end, we'd become very close friends. But in all the time I'd known her, she'd always been the consummate professional, always dressed for the job at hand. This was a side of her I'd never seen before—and a side that was very distracting.

"So, this is Rene's—er, Victor's boat?" I asked.

"He's aboard *Wind Dancer*," she replied, not looking up. "We didn't want to take the chance that there was a hidden tracking device on board, so we switched boats."

Ahead lay nothing but water for more than an hour. Far in the distance, I could just make out the flash of green light at four second intervals from Harbor Key. Aboard the *Revenge*, we'd have been there in just a few minutes. The light was low on the horizon, so I knew it was no more than ten miles away.

I tried to remain focused on the horizon. It wasn't easy, with five-feet-ten-inches of beautifully tanned and shapely blond femininity just feet away.

Charity still hadn't explained why she didn't trust Stockwell, but I knew she'd get to that in her own time. She'd sailed over a thousand miles to get here.

"I can find out," I offered. "In a back-handed kind of way, of course. What's this boat's draft, anyway?"

Arching her back so she could turn and tilt her head back to see me, she said, "Six feet. Can you do that? Without anyone knowing why you're asking?"

"Shouldn't be a problem. Next time I talk to Stockwell, I'll just ask him how long it'll be before you get here. If he has any kind of tracking on your boat, he'll tell me. And if that doesn't get me anywhere ... well, Chyrel works for Deuce now."

"She's ex-CIA," Charity said, turning her face forward again. "I like her; she's always been very nice toward me. But with them, you can never tell where their allegiance lies."

I left that alone. Chyrel Koshinski had worked for the Agency, that was true. But she'd been with Deuce's team

"Not a problem," I said, switching off the light and stepping out of the shower, my clean towel around my waist. "There's hot water in here."

I dressed quickly in my old clothes and went to the front door. When I opened it, Charity was standing there with a towel wrapped around her, which barely reached the top of her thighs.

"Go ahead," I said, pointing toward the other door to the head as I stepped back to let her in. "You're cooking, you get the first shower."

"Thanks," she said, striding past me and padding barefoot to the head, clean clothes rolled up under her arm. She looked back over her shoulder. "I'm really sorry I startled you. On the boat, I rarely wear clothes after dark."

She turned the knob and went into the head. With just the towel covering her body, her legs looked impossibly long. I forced myself to look away and went over to one of the recliners by the big, south-facing window and looked out.

Rene, or whatever his name was, did have a really beautiful boat. I knew it was fiberglass, but it resembled older wooden vessels, with a high bow and long bowsprit. Seeing it sitting there, tied to my pier, with nothing else around but a few small mangrove-covered islands, it was easy to allow my mind to look back in time. I imagined how all the Keys looked when the only way to get to these ancient coral and limestone outcroppings was by sail. Harbor Channel, and probably even my little island, might have been a hiding place for privateers.

From the small table between the recliners, I picked up a book I'd been reading off and on, switched on the light, and sat down. It was a biography about John "Mad Dog" Mattis, a Marine general who'd just been appointed Commanding General of United States Joint Forces Command. A colorful character, to say the least.

Alone, I thought again, as I tried to make sense of the words I was reading. The distraction was too great and I laid the book on the table beside the chair. *Alone for at least a couple of days. With a beautiful woman who likes to go around naked.*

I rarely get my signals right when it comes to women, particularly those who are more than a decade younger. A man doesn't know whether to be the responsible, older brother, or just act presidential and toss them in a hot tub filled with key lime sauce.

Taking Mac's phone from my pocket, I flipped it open. I'd expected him to retrieve it by now. I scrolled through his contact list. Like mine, it was very small. Halfway through, a familiar name jumped out: Mel Woodson, Mac's girlfriend. She used to be an environmental lawyer in DC and Mac had worked for her dad until he died. Wood and Mac had built or worked on a lot of bridges throughout the Keys.

I took a chance and clicked the *call* button. It rang a couple of times, before Mel answered.

"Mac?"

I didn't know exactly what or how much to say. "Mel, it's Jesse."

"McDermitt?"

"Yes, ma'am," I replied. "I have Mac's phone and some info for him."

She didn't respond for a moment, and I thought I'd lost the signal. They'd added a new cell tower on Big Pine Key

CHAPTER EIGHT

Tony Jacobs sat alone at the bar in the hotel lounge. Two women sat at a table watching a big screen TV. After texting Jesse, he called Deuce and told him he was going to just hang around for a bit. Carmichael had struck him as a drinking man, and would probably hit the bar sooner rather than later.

"The man does have a nose for things that shine," Deuce said. "If Jesse thinks this guy has a stash of stolen jewels, he probably does. Don't stay out too late, though. Your new wife will be pissed at me."

The bar was L-shaped, and Tony was sitting next to a large potted palm at the far end, near where the bar joined the wall. "I got a feeling this guy will hit the bar within an hour," Tony said, then saw Carmichael enter the dimly lit lounge and pause to let his eyes adjust. "Scratch that. He just walked in."

The man looked around, sizing up the few people in the place. He paused on the two young women sitting together at a table, lingering longer than would be considered polite, then his eyes shifted toward the end of the bar. Tony saw this through his peripheral vision, but kept his eyes glued to the TV at the other end of the bar, which was showing an NFL game.

Tony had his half-drunk, glazed, and bored businessman face on. Those who went to bed in a different city every night, staying in hotels near where they were conducting their business, had a distinct look. They'd seen just about everything and been nearly everywhere, so little interested them anymore.

The man took a seat at the corner of the bar. From where he sat, he could see himself and what was behind him in the mirror. Tony glanced at Carmichael as the bigger man scraped his stool on the floor. He nodded, as is the polite thing for a person to do in a public place when thrust together by chance.

Carmichael nodded back, dismissing him, as if accepting him as exactly what Tony wanted him to—a bored traveler. The bartender came over and took the man's order, then glanced at Tony. Tony waved him off. He still had half a drink in front of him, the other half having been poured discreetly into the potted plant beside him.

Pretending to watch the game again, Tony could just see the man out of the corner of his eye. Carmichael was staring intently at the two women again. Tony calculated that he was an inch or two taller than Tony's own five-nine, and though the man outweighed him by a good fifteen pounds, he didn't carry it well. Tony guessed him to be in his early thirties, maybe a year or two younger than himself, but he looked like he'd given in to drink

CHAPTER NINE

I didn't sleep a whole lot. The wind picked up a little just before midnight, and the clanking of the halyard on Charity's boat and the gentle creaking of her fenders against my dock was a constant reminder that she was out there. And probably naked.

When the east-facing window in my bedroom began to show the first faint light of dawn creeping in, I threw off the sheet and went to my hanging closet. I pulled on a clean pair of well-worn jeans, grabbed a long-sleeved work shirt, and went into the living room. I was planning to fly up to Miami to have a look at this Wilson Carmichael in person. Octobers don't get very cold in the Keys, but at a higher altitude it would be a little chilly.

Thrusting my right hand through the shirt sleeve, I grabbed the doorknob and opened the door to let Finn out, still struggling to get my left arm in its sleeve.

Charity was standing just outside the door. "Good morning," she said, as Finn sniffed her hand then ran down the back steps. She was dressed in khaki shorts and a red tank top, both of which accentuated her deeply tanned skin, reminding me instantly of her lack of tan lines.

"Thanks for dinner last night," I said, stepping out and closing the door behind me. "It's been a while since I had a steak."

"You're welcome," she said. "I love a good steak. Have you thought about how you're going to ask Director Stockwell?"

"I did, as a matter of fact." I turned toward the back deck. "I'm flying up to Miami, and I'll call him when I'm in the air. I'll say I just flew over a boat that looks like yours, and ask him if he's heard from you."

"You know what kind of boat the *Dancer* is?" she asked.

"He told me once that it was an antique sailboat designed by John Alden. Aren't many of those on the water, I bet."

"That might work." She fell in beside me as I followed Finn to the back steps. "What can I do around here while you're gone?"

"The keys to the little Grady-White are in it," I replied, "as are the keys to my flats skiff. The fob on any of the boats' keyrings will open the door. Catch something fresh, and I'll grill it for dinner."

"That, I can do," she said, as we walked down the back steps to the clearing. "Is this guy dangerous? Want me to come with you?"

"No to both," I said, laughing. "I'm old, but I ain't dead yet. And, from what I gather, you need some decompressing time. Mother Ocean is good for that."

"Ocean is my potion, I need vitamin sea," she sang.

"So, you hang out here and relax," I said. "I'll be back before dark. Nobody is scheduled to come up here until next weekend, and by now people know to schedule ahead.

Taking my old phone out, I turned it back on and stuck it in my pocket. I'd resisted, but was now becoming a slave to the little box of electronic wizardry. I flew farther out over the water, and as I approached Key Largo I contacted Miami Approach Control for landing instructions. They put me in the pattern, two miles behind a twin-engine commuter. I banked west on the downwind leg.

My phone vibrated in my pocket, startling me. I fished it out and looked at the screen. I had a text message from Devon.

Slow day. Want to get lunch?

Fumbling with the thing one-handed, I managed to type the word *Flying*, and sent it.

It vibrated again, almost immediately. *Where?*

Miami.

Call me when you land, came the instant reply.

I replied with just the letters *OK*. I don't see how people can type a message so fast on those things. For that matter, it makes no sense to me why, if a person held a telephone in their hand and wanted to convey an idea to someone, they wouldn't just call and talk to them. Instead, a hundred billion alphabet streams fly through the airwaves every day.

Following the Cessna in the pattern was uneventful. I thought about why Charity would be suspicious of Stockwell. There was no doubt that Victor Pitt was a paranoid man, always looking over his shoulder. Whether he had reason to or not, didn't make him any less suspicious of others. If Charity had been spending time with him, some of his paranoia might have rubbed off, but I had no idea what communications might have gone back and forth between her and Stockwell. She might have picked up something from what he'd said that caused her to not trust him.

Once I had the *Hopper* on the ground and had taxied to a parking area, I shut down the engine and went through my post-flight checklist. Walking toward the general aviation terminal, I remembered my promise to call Devon.

"I thought you hated Miami," she said, by way of hello.

"I do," I replied. "I'm working on a case with Deuce."

There was silence on the other end for a second. "Is it dangerous?"

"That's the reason I came up here. To find out." Then, to change the subject, I asked, "Why are you bored?"

"The leads we got yesterday didn't pan out," she said. "We're dead in the water again. When will you be home?"

"Sorry to hear that," I said, genuinely concerned. Devon took her work very seriously—even personally—at times. "I'm not planning to spend the night and should make it back to the island by dark. I just touched down and I'm heading into the terminal to arrange fuel."

"Okay, I'll let you go."

"I'll give you a call when I get home," I said, then told her goodbye and ended the call.

As I walked through the FBO terminal, it suddenly struck me as odd that Devon hadn't asked anything more about Charity. I went to the Signature Flight Support desk and gave them my debit card to pay for fueling the *Hopper*. After running it, the girl at the desk handed it back and I continued outside. Like most fixed-base operators, they would take care of the fueling and charge the fuel to my card, along with a small service fee.

There was a single cab waiting outside the general aviation terminal. I opened the door and got in the back seat.

completely unbuttoned, and she had a large bag over her right shoulder.

She smiled at the bartender as she walked toward me. It wasn't until she stopped at the corner of the bar that I realized it was Chyrel. She ordered a Coke, and when the bartender went to the other end of the bar to get it, she turned toward me.

"What are you staring at?" she whispered, her Alabama accent dripping with Confederate jasmine.

"What the hell are you doing?" I asked, after the bartender left her drink and retreated to his newspaper.

"Relax, Jesse. Deuce said he wanted a listening device close to a redneck hanging out by the pool." She looked out over the deck, surveying the people there. "Ball cap and jeans, right?"

"That's our man," Tony said.

"Ha, those bimbos don't stand a chance," she said, sliding a small black case toward me. Then she took her Coke and walked slowly toward the door.

Chyrel had always seemed the nerdy type, but outgoing and very friendly. Seeing so much of her at one time, I realized there was more to her than first met the eye. She paused at the door to put her sunglasses back on, then pushed it open and strode out into the sunlight, like a supermodel on a catwalk.

Outside, she moved slowly and seductively around the end of the pool. Nearly every man out there turned to look at her, even an obviously gay couple. She was right; most of the women fawning over Carmichael and his money were younger than Chyrel by eight or ten years, and their inexperience showed in the way they moved and acted.

Chyrel slowly walked around the pool, pretending to check the direction of the sun, before settling on a chaise lounge that was ten feet from Carmichael and his entourage. Satisfied that the chair provided a direct exposure to the bright sun, she placed her bag next to it, and shrugged out of her shirt.

Carmichael made no effort to hide the fact that he'd noticed her, and stared as he waved the poolside waiter over. He said something to the young man, who nodded and went over to where Chyrel was removing her wrap.

I picked up the little box she'd given me and opened it. Inside were two earwigs. I took one and slid the box to Tony, then turned the device on and put in in my ear. The miniature transceivers were very small and flesh-colored, so they were barely noticeable, especially now that my hair was down over my ears.

"Give the gentleman my thanks," I heard Chyrel say. "But I already have a Coke, and one is all I allow myself." With that, she sat on the lounge chair and turned, stretching her legs out slowly as she lay back.

The waiter went back to Carmichael and said something to him, then continued to the bar to fill other orders. Carmichael pulled his shades down his nose and looked over them at Chyrel, who was ignoring him completely.

Over the earwig, I could hear an occasional yelp or splash, but couldn't make out anything anyone said. After a moment, Carmichael stood, brushed past two women vying for his attention, and walked over to Chyrel. I turned and started toward the door.

"She's got it," Tony said, stopping me.

"My apologies," I barely heard Carmichael say, as he sat in a chair beside Chyrel. His accent was Midwestern,

CHAPTER TEN

A s Chyrel and I started through the bar to the lobby, there was a clicking sound in my earwig, and Deuce's voice came over it. "I don't know what you stumbled into, Jesse. What the hell was that all about?"

"Are you still recording?" Chyrel asked.

"Yeah," Deuce replied. "Paul's still listening live, and he'll break in if anything interesting comes up."

"The Hispanic woman is following you," Tony said, as we crossed the bar toward him.

"Shit," Deuce said. "Paul just told me that Carmichael told her to find out what room you're in. You guys can't just leave and you can't hang out at the bar."

"Got it covered," Chyrel said, taking my arm and hurrying toward the lobby. "I hacked into their computer before coming up here, just in case. We have a suite available to us—open ended."

We exited the lounge just as the Hispanic woman came into it from the opposite door.

"Give the desk clerk your coke dealer name," Chyrel said. "Tell him you forgot your key card. We're in suite nine-fifteen."

A moment later, armed with a key card, Chyrel and I got on the elevator. "She's waiting for the next elevator," Tony's voice informed us over the comm. "And watching yours to see which floor you're getting off on."

"Let's make sure she knows," I said, as the elevator door opened. "Getting off on nine now."

Chyrel and I started down the hall to the left, and Tony informed us the woman was getting on the other elevator.

"Moving toward the suite," I said, walking with Chyrel down the long hallway. "I don't have a clue what these people are into besides having stolen something. You come up with anything on Carmichael?"

"Nothing jumped out at me," Chyrel replied, stopping in front of room nine-twelve. She knelt and placed a small listening device on the floor outside the door, then activated it.

Taking a narrow black rod from her oversized purse, she telescoped it out to four feet and pushed the bug under the door and to the left, until she hit something.

"His military history looks clean and boring," she said, putting the rod away as we hurried down the hall. "I couldn't find anything at all prior to that. Deuce, bug number two is three feet inside his room. It's against the wall, probably right next to the bathroom door jamb, or maybe a table leg."

In front of room nine-fifteen, I swiped the card and pushed the door open, holding it with my foot. When the elevator chimed its arrival, Chyrel stood up on her toes, and threw her arms around my neck, as the elevator opened.

turned it around to show us a still from the surveillance camera in the hall, and a mug shot from Nogales, Arizona. Part of the snake tattoo was clearly visible on the shoulder of the woman in the mug shot.

"Rosana Cruz," Chyrel continued. "Panamanian, living mostly in Nogales, Arizona. Several arrests; drugs, mostly."

"That's her, all right," I said.

"What do you guys think?" Deuce asked.

"We need to get a permanent bug inside that room," Tony replied. "There's a whole lot we don't know."

"What they were talking about is just sick," Chyrel said. "And I get the feeling that they've done this before."

"A few minutes of talking to him would confirm it, but I'd bet that Carmichael suffers from classic narcissistic personality disorder," Paul said. "And the woman is his perfect counter-part, histrionic personality disorder."

"I know that first one," Tony said.

Paul sat forward in his chair. "The narcissist lacks empathy for others. A person with HPD will constantly seek the attention of others. They won't get that from the narcissist, making them try even harder. It will usually manifest itself in inappropriate seductive behavior."

"Back home in Mobile," Chyrel said, "we have a real simple word for that: a slut."

Andrew looked down at me from where he stood beside the driver's seat. "What was it that put them on your radar, Gunny?"

I didn't even have to think about it. I knew and trusted these people like they were my own family. "He stole a chest full of emeralds from the widow of a soldier killed in Ecuador. The soldier had apparently bartered for them, and hid them in a concrete post by the back steps of the house they're building. Carmichael had served with the dead soldier and learned about the emeralds somehow, then came down here to help her out."

"We don't have troops in Ecuador," Paul said. "At least not that I'm aware of."

"He was an engineer," I explained. "Surveying possible locations for a new base in Central or South America."

"I have to ask," Deuce said. "Not that we won't do what needs to be done to stop these whackos, but will there be a payday in this?"

"Probably not," I said. "But I'll cover all expenses. The widow's a Conch, trying to finish a house she and her late husband were building. And she's about eight months pregnant."

"I'm in," Andrew said, his deep baritone voice practically echoing in the van. He'd lost his wife and only son in the terrorist attacks on 9/11 and I knew he had a soft spot where mothers and children were concerned.

"Me too," Tony and Chyrel said at the same time.

"Whatever it takes," Paul chimed in.

"Then we're unanimous," Deuce added. "How do we want to handle it? If we bring in the police, the widow can kiss the emeralds goodbye. What they're planning is way past theft."

"Then we get the emeralds back first," I said. "The widow's gonna need a payday. Then we can decide whether or not to bring in the police."

"You know what this sounds like?" Andrew asked.

Tony nodded his head solemnly. "Merc work."

"Actually," the burly Coast Guardsman said, with a laugh, "I was thinking of John D. MacDonald's first Travis McGee

"Oh," I said, not wanting to talk about her. "Yeah, I guess she is."

"And very young."

"Yeah," I replied, striving for something innocent to say. "That, too. Kim seems to like her. They're not all that far apart in age."

Kim is the youngest of my two daughters from my first marriage. Her mother took them away when I was suddenly deployed to Panama. Since I was unable to attend the divorce proceedings, her lawyer got her full custody with very limited and supervised visitation. Then she'd moved them hundreds of miles away so that I couldn't see them.

Kim had come to the Keys to find me, and had become a semi-permanent semi-Conch, splitting her time between my island and her studies at University of Florida.

"Jesse McDermitt!" Devon said. When I looked at her, she had her feet planted and her hands on her hips. "That woman is nowhere near Kim's age. If anything, she's just a few years younger than me."

Unable to help myself, I grinned and walked toward her, taking her hands in my own. "Do I detect a bit of jealousy?"

"You're out here, miles from anyone and anywhere, alone with her? Overnight! And you lied about who she was."

"I apologize about that. Charity asked me to keep her whereabouts and identity a secret for now. She has some issues to work out and only needs someone she trusts to listen to her."

Devon moved into my arms, the warmth of her body lighting a fire in my belly. "I know nothing went on. You're not the type. But I can't help but feel a little threatened; all men are weak."

I kissed her lightly and she pressed her body closer, returning my kiss. My arms encircled her narrow waist, and I let my hands drift up under her blouse, feeling the warmth of her bare back where it curved inward.

Charity returned with the fish, along with some peppers, tomatoes, and wild onions from the garden. "You guys go watch the sunset," she said, placing two cast iron skillets over the flames in the stone barbecue pit. "I'm too hungry to wait for a potato to cook, so I'll do a stir fry."

"Are you sure you don't need any help?" Devon asked.

Charity didn't even look up from her dicing, just waved us away. I took Devon's hand and led her out to the north pier, where we could see the sun setting over Content Passage and Little Crane Key.

We sat down in our usual spot, Devon leaning against my shoulder, her hand massaging my thigh. "Are we ever going to be able to have a normal life, like everyone else?"

I turned and kissed her temple, where the wispy little hairs curled back over her ear. "Define normal."

"You know," she said. "Regular nine-to-five jobs, a house with a car in the driveway."

"I have to leave at first light," I said. Probably not what she wanted to hear. "I need to take the *Hopper* back to Marathon and rent a flashy car to go back up to Miami."

"This case you're working on? Should the law be involved?"

"Eventually," I said. "We have to recover something that was stolen first."

"Which is exactly what law enforcement does," she said, a concerned look in her eye.

"I can't tell you everything just yet," I said, choosing my words carefully. "The theft is just the tip of the iceberg, but

CHAPTER
ELEVEN

I t was still dark outside, but I guessed sunrise would be coming soon. Devon had drifted back off to sleep an hour earlier, after another boisterous round of lovemaking. Her head lay on my shoulder, and my arm around her was numb.

I'd been lying in bed thinking about where our relationship was headed. That wasn't something I'd done much pondering over in the past. Quite a few women had come into and out of my life since Sandy left with the girls, nineteen years before. Things got very busy for me after she left, with multiple deployments to the Middle East and embassy duty in Somalia, so I didn't really have much of a social life.

An incident in Mogadishu had ended with my being transferred back to Camp Lejeune as a sniper instructor. It also nixed any chance of advancement beyond Gunnery Sergeant, and I retired from the Corps five years later.

While at Lejeune, I met a woman in a bar, and we got married a month later. Big mistake. I'd been so busy in the previous four years that I hadn't had time for dating, and fell hard for the first woman who let me into her bed. It only lasted nine months.

After leaving the Corps and settling in the Keys, there'd been a succession of women, mostly just flings with tourists. None of those had developed into any kind of relationship.

Then I'd met Alex. Alex had been my soul mate in many ways, but she'd been murdered on our wedding night. When I lost her, I thought I'd never find happiness again. There had been a few women in the three years since, but fate always seemed to devise a plan to move them out of my life.

Would the same thing happen with Devon?

I looked at her asleep beside me, unsure how I felt about her. Being older—and hopefully wiser—I no longer rushed into things. Slow is smooth, and smooth is fast; that was the mantra of house-to-house fighting in the sandbox, Iraq and Afghanistan. With some things, moving too fast means doing it over.

The air was dry and cool, the front having finally arrived in the middle of the night. It rarely gets cold here in the Keys, but occasionally a front that dumps snow in Dallas or Atlanta will push far enough south to make the mercury fall into the fifties here. This time of year, it only brought cold rain to those places, and the change in temperature here was slight, but noticeable.

I brought my mind back to the task at hand. The car would be the hard part. There were plenty of rental places in both Marathon and Miami. But a Civic or Prius wasn't

I kissed her as Charity climbed into the co-pilot's seat. "Are you sure?" She nodded, and I hugged her tightly. "He has food in—oh hell, you know where everything is. Thank you so much."

Climbing into the aft cabin, I handed Devon's bag back to her, kissed her again, and made my way to the cockpit. Devon untied the lines from the pontoon cleats and held the wing strut, while I did a quick pre-flight and started the big radial engine.

Idling away from the dock, I waved back at her and Finn, both now sitting on the edge of the pier. She waved back and smiled. It struck me that there weren't many women who would insist that their man fly off with a beautiful young woman, volunteer to dog-sit while he was gone, then smile and wave good-bye.

Switching to the Unicom frequency, I announced my intent and position, then switched to Miami Center and requested a VFR flight plan to Miami International.

"Not the *Rusty Anchor*?" Charity asked.

"No need," I replied. "We can rent a better car in Miami."

Miami Center advised me of weather conditions in Miami and wished me a pleasant flight. The sun was rising, but it was hidden behind big burnt-orange clouds. The report didn't mention any bad weather, but the *red sky at night* mantra echoed in my head.

Minutes later, the pontoons broke free of the water and we climbed into the sky. I banked slowly toward the southeast to pick up US-1 and was awed at the horizon, streaked with pastel shades of red, orange, pink, and yellow.

At three thousand feet, I leveled off and turned to follow the highway north. I switched the intercom on, so Charity and I could talk and still hear ATC if I needed to.

"Beautiful sunrise," Charity said. "I'd choose to stay in port, seeing that. But this plane's a lot faster than my boat."

"Wanna take the yoke?"

She didn't hesitate, taking the second wheel immediately. "My aircraft."

"Your aircraft," I said, raising my hands from the main wheel on the Y-shaped yoke.

I'd noticed when we'd flown down to Key West that she'd studied the instruments on the fifty-five-year-old plane, and checked them constantly while in flight.

Charity glanced at the dash for only a second, now that she was familiar with the gauges. "Don't be surprised if you come home to find drapes and doilies in your house," she said.

"Devon's not like that," I said.

"Ha!"

"She's not," I insisted. "She's a cop and, before that, a Marine."

Charity smiled over at me. "She's a girly girl—but, other than that, a perfect match for you, and every man's fantasy."

"A girly girl?"

Charity studied my face for a moment. "You really don't know, do you?"

"Know what?"

She grinned. "Your girlfriend is a switch-hitter."

"What the hell are you talking about?"

Her grin broadened. "Devon is bisexual."

"She is not," I retorted. "And just how would you know, anyway?"

Charity looked forward, through the windshield, as the *Hopper* droned onward. "She is," she replied, with an air of

men sat down in the other three swivel chairs, and Deuce and I stood at either end.

"Are you back to stay?" Chyrel asked Charity, once I'd closed the back door.

Charity looked at Deuce, and he nodded. "You have a place here," he said, "whenever and for how long you want. Colonel Stockwell expedited the paperwork, and we're all civilian employees of our own private security firm."

Paul extended his right hand to Charity. "I'm Paul," he said. "Paul Bender, former Chicago police detective."

"And the former head of the Secret Service's presidential protection detail," I added. "Paul holds a PhD in criminal psychology."

She shook Paul's hand then looked at Deuce. "Jesse told me a little about what you're doing. I'd like to help if you'll have me, but I can't make any promises going forward."

Deuce glanced across the van at me, and I gave him a slight nod. "You have a place here for however long you want to stay," he said, then turned to Chyrel. "Tell them what you found out."

Chyrel turned toward her computer screen, her hands dancing across the keyboard. A picture of a soldier came on one of the four monitors in front of her.

"This is the late Captain Dan Huggins, United States Army. He was an engineer officer, and led a team of enlisted technical engineers—five men altogether—to survey possible locations for military bases in Central and South America."

"What kind of soldier was he?" I asked, knowing that Chyrel had a penchant for reading between the lines of a service record book.

She shrugged. "Average. Nothing at all about his service jumped out at me. He was neither an outstanding leader, nor a slacker. He seemed to do his job and little more."

"Nothing?" Deuce asked.

Chyrel smiled. "There are several gaps in his jacket," she said. "Times where, apparently, he wasn't doing anything at all. No work reports, no physical fitness reports, no pro and con marks noted... nothing. This made me curious, so I started digging."

"Uh-oh," Tony muttered, winking at Charity.

"I finally got a hit through facial recognition," Chyrel said, smiling at me. "Your Captain Huggins was with the CIA."

"Are you sure?" Deuce asked.

"Yeah, one of the photos that came up was taken at a bank in Bogata. Captain Huggins was talking to an operative I recognized from many years ago, another CIA computer analyst turned field agent, so I took a stroll through some computers in Langley. He was definitely a spook."

Another screen came to life, showing a picture of Carmichael.

"This is former Staff Sergeant Wilson Carmichael. He was part of Captain Huggins's team—a combat engineer with a prior MOS as a watercraft operator. The rest of the team were all construction tech guys, and had all worked with Huggins in the past. Carmichael was the only one of the team that was new, and he was the only one to come back from Ecuador alive, this past July."

"How were the other soldiers killed?" Charity asked.

"Three were shot in the back," Chyrel replied. "Execution style. Huggins was shot in the head. Carmichael wasn't with them when the bandits attacked, he was shacked up

"Good to know," I said, then turned toward Chyrel. "I don't suppose that bug can access his computer, can it."

"Unfortunately, no," she replied, "but that's not really a problem. I can get into the hotel's internet server easy enough, and pull up anything he looks at on the web."

"Deuce said you came up with a plan?"

When the bartender brought my drink, I neglected to pay for it and walked over to a chair in the shade, directly in front of Carmichael. I wanted the bartender to come to me while I was sitting, to get the money for the drink. I settled into the chair, took a sip from the drink, and stretched out to wait.

"Excuse me, sir," a voice said near my shoulder.

Opening my eyes, I turned my head. The bartender was standing next to me.

"You forgot to pay for your drink, sir. Would you like me to put it on your room tab?"

I hadn't even thought of that. A chance to kill two birds with one stone. "Yeah," I replied, gruffly. "Room nine-fifteen. Buchannan." He turned and started back to the bar. "Wait," I called after him, fishing into my pocket for my money clip. I peeled off a ten and handed it to the bartender. "A little stronger next time, huh?"

He smiled and took the bill. "Of course, Mister Buchannan."

As the bartender left, I saw both Carmichael and Cruz watching me. A woman in a bikini walked past my chair and I let my eyes stray after her, as I put the money clip back into my pocket.

Pulling my hand out, I made sure the handkerchief with the emerald came with it. The handkerchief unrolled as it fell onto the deck and the bright green stone rolled free, just as I'd hoped it would. I quickly scooped both up with my left hand and stuffed them back into my pocket.

"Smooth," I heard Paul say over my earwig. He'd preceded me to the deck and was sitting at the far side of the bar, watching. Then he chuckled softly. "He bit. And her eyes nearly bugged out of her head."

I continued to avoid looking in Carmichael's direction and leaned my head back in the chair, once more closing my eyes. It was noon and the sun was directly overhead. I was over-dressed for the pool, in jeans and a denim shirt. But the air was cool, so I wasn't uncomfortable.

"Excuse me," a woman said, from somewhere near my feet. "Aren't you with Ginger?"

I opened my eyes to see Rosana Cruz standing in front of me. I smiled the smile of the drunk womanizer as I lowered my sunglasses and looked at her from head to toe. "You know Ginger?"

"I met her yesterday," Cruz lied. "Here at the pool. Then you came and picked her up. Are the two of you staying here, too?"

"For a few days," I said, putting my shades back on and nodding at the seat next to me. "We were planning to go cruising with a friend of hers, but the guy's boat is broke down. We were gonna go to the Bahamas early next week and spend a month there. Not sure if it's gonna happen now."

"That's a shame," Cruz said, sitting on the edge of the chair next to me and putting a hand on my knee. "Me and a bunch of friends are going to the Bahamas, too. If your plans don't work out, maybe you could join us?"

Looking over at her, I took another sip of the watered-down tourist rum, and spoke with a drunk's long-winded slur. "I kinda doubt it. This whole thing was Ginger's idea. A pirate treasure hunt. I'd just as soon get back to the farm in Illinois. Snow's forecast next week, and I don't completely trust my foreman to make sure all the livestock gets fed and stays warm if I ain't there."

his shaded table. The young woman that had been sitting with the two of them moved her chair around to make room for us.

"I understand you're looking for a charter to the Bahamas," Carmichael said, extending his hand. "Wilson's the name."

"Buchannan," I said, shaking his hand. "But friends just call me Stretch."

His grip told me there was more to him than met the eye. Up close, I could see the corded muscle of powerful forearms.

"Wilson's the first name," he said. It didn't slip past me that neither he nor Cruz had given me their last names.

"I'm not really looking to charter," I said. "My wife and I came down to go on a cruise with a friend and his boat's in the shop."

Carmichael sat forward and took a pull from his drink. "You know how to drive a boat?"

"Powerboat?" I replied. "Sure, but I'm not a sailor."

"My boat's a big trawler. Not fast, but very reliable and sturdy. We'll be gone two weeks. First stop is the Berry Islands, ever heard of them?"

"Can't say as I have," I lied.

"A hundred and thirty nautical miles from here," Carmichael said. "It'll take twenty straight hours to get there, and I could use a good man to spell me at the helm for a little shut-eye."

"Two weeks?" I asked. "How much of the Bahamas can you see in that time?"

Carmichael sat back and drained his drink, motioning the bartender with his finger, circling it around the table to order another round.

"Not a whole lot," he said. "The Bahamas are more than seven-hundred islands scattered over almost two-hundred-thousand square miles of ocean. But I know quite a few outta the way anchorages where we can party hearty, and there won't be anyone else around for miles."

I pretended to consider it a moment. "How many are going?" I finally asked.

"Me and Wilson," Cruz replied. "And Diane here, and her boyfriend, plus two other girls."

"Three men and five women? Must be a pretty big boat." I reached across to shake hands with Diane, a tiny woman with glasses who reminded me of the librarian at my junior high school. "Pleased to meet you, Diane. Your boyfriend doesn't know much about boats?"

"We're newlyweds, actually" Diane replied demurely. She couldn't have been more than five feet tall. She wore a baggy, long-sleeved blouse, unbuttoned to the top of her bikini top, and loose-fitting khaki pants. Though I couldn't see much of her, I was pretty sure she wouldn't tip the scale into three digits.

"She'll sleep fourteen, easy," Carmichael went on to say. "Be nice if we could find a few more people to go along, preferably the eye candy variety. Know anyone looking to have a little fun?"

I couldn't help but notice that the man's eyes kept straying to Diane's open blouse. He also didn't try to hide it, which I could see made Diane uncomfortable. In fact, Carmichael stared brazenly at every passing bikini or skirt.

"No, we're not from around here," I said, then an idea came to me. "There's one unattached woman in our group. She seems to be a little bored with Miami. And I know she can handle a boat."

his twenties and thirties, dragging the same wife and kids from one post to another, but if you get a star on your shoulder by the time you're forty, and the kiddies are grown and gone, you can trade her in for a newer model."

"What a degenerate dirtbag," I heard Chyrel say.

"I like Jesse's term better," Charity said from the van two blocks behind us. "Turd fondler."

I almost laughed, but managed to control it, and played along with Carmichael. "Wouldn't know, I was never in the Army. But wouldn't a *trophy wife* be a woman who marries the older guy for money?"

"Usually, yeah," Carmichael replied. "That ain't the case with you and Ginger?"

We'd rehearsed our backgrounds and I was hoping he'd ask about it. "Hardly. I was doing okay when we met, been divorced five years and not looking. My farm is forty thousand acres of the best bottom land on the Ohio River."

"That explains the car," he said. "I never been in an Italian car before. So, your wife's richer than you?"

Asking someone you just met what their net worth is was something that usually didn't happen, at least not in the social circles I was in—not that my sphere of friends was all that large. But I'd met others that didn't have that filter and knew how to play along.

"Her dad was a lawyer and later a judge. He'd been buying tech stocks in her name since she was born; one of the first to buy into Microsoft when they went public. He sent her to Auburn, where she graduated with a degree in computer science. Her dad died later that year and she sold her stocks just before the tech bubble burst seven years ago. She's worth a lot more than me."

"Turn in right up here," Carmichael said, pointing ahead and to the left. "Where it says *Mistrall's*."

I parked the car and we got out. I didn't expect Andrew and Tony to arrive any time soon, but I took a slow look around out of habit.

"You think this Gabby can afford to take some time off for an extended cruise?" Carmichael asked, as we walked toward the front of the store.

"No idea," I replied. "About all I know is that she owns a sailing yacht and doesn't have anyone to answer to."

We entered the front of the store. Shelves full of various boat parts and optional equipment extended at right angles to both sides of the center aisle.

"Hey, Mister Mistrall," Carmichael said, as we approached the counter. "I need to go aboard and fetch something, if you don't mind."

"Meaning you want to see how the work's coming along?" the old man said, looking over his reading glasses, and setting his paper aside. "Customers aren't usually allowed in the work area, but you happened to come at lunch time. Sure, come on back. I think you're gonna be really happy, Mister Carmichael."

The man visibly winced at the mention of his last name. It was apparently something he didn't want me to know.

"This is my friend, Stretch."

The old man nodded to me, and opened the door to a shop area in the back of the building. We followed him through the door. The shop was completely open at the far end, with three boats on the hard, under cover. One I recognized immediately as James's old salvage boat.

"Bottom's all finished up," Mistrall said, as we approached the dark blue hull. "They were doing demo work in the

My throat felt raw and hot, and my eyes were itchy. Suddenly, I wasn't as steady on my feet as I usually was, and a fog seemed to envelop my brain. Carmichael laughed and patted me on the shoulder as I coughed. I felt like one of my lungs was about to become dislodged.

"I bet the weed you get on the farm ain't quite as good as what they get around here," Carmichael said.

"You got that right," I replied. "Nothing even close."

Getting the cough under control, I stood on wobbly legs, the confined interior of the cabin seeming to close in.

"There's one other thing," Carmichael said, putting the pipe in the box and storing it back in the cabinet.

"What's that?"

"Out at the pool?" he began. "You dropped something green and shiny out of your pocket."

My hand instinctively went to my pants pocket, and I pulled out the handkerchief with the emerald rolled up inside. I unrolled it and extended the stone to him. I wanted him to have a good look at it, to see for sure that it was identical. "You mean this?"

Carmichael took the emerald and went over to the main hatch, where the shop lights shined in. The light reflected off the surfaces of the many faceted sides, sending beams of green light around the salon, to make green dots and dashes wherever it came into contact with the boat's interior.

"That's one big-ass emerald," he said, handing it back.

"Don't know anything about them," I lied, folding it back into my pocket. "Ginger found it on a treasure hunt that her friend has every year. He hides them all over an island for his guests to find. From what he says, it might be worth a few hundred bucks, but it ain't no diamond."

A noise from above preceded a shadow, then a man stepped down from the cockpit. He was obviously one of the workmen, dressed in jeans and long sleeves, with a ball cap sitting backward on his head, a surgical mask perched on the front of it.

Sniffing the air, he looked blankly at both of us. "One of you guys the owner?"

"Yeah," Carmichael said. "I'm the owner."

"We hit a coupla snags, during the demo," the man said, unconcerned about the pot smoking. "Things we need to talk about before continuing the build. You got a few minutes where I can go over them with you?"

"Sure," Carmichael replied. "In fact, my friend here gave me an idea that I want you guys to add to the work order." Turning to me, Carmichael said, "Think you can find your way back, amigo?"

"Yeah, sure," I replied, feeling slightly sluggish. "I can get back okay." I didn't understand it; I'd seen Jimmy smoke a number of joints, one after the other. He called them spliffs, or hog legs. An exceptionally fat one he called a *zeppelin*, but why I was remembering that just now, I had no idea. Pot didn't seem to affect him much more than a beer There must be some kind of tolerance built up through habitual use.

As I slowly mounted the steps to the cockpit, my legs felt very heavy. I carefully moved over onto the ladder and descended. A few minutes later, I was out in the sunlight, walking toward the car.

"Did I just hear you smoking weed?" Tony asked.

"I think he was testing me," I replied, unlocking the door, and getting in. The inside of the car was very hot,

CHAPTER
FOURTEEN

The door opened and Charity came in, followed by Tony and Andrew. Them having key cards didn't surprise me in the least. I was sure that among the many devices Chyrel carried in her electronics bag all the time, she'd be bound to have something that could duplicate the magnetic strip on the back of a hotel key card.

"Chyrel was about to tell us about more unsolved murders near Army bases," I said, as Charity dropped several shopping bags on the bed nearest the door.

Deuce and Chyrel went on to explain what they'd learned again, since the others had had their comms disconnected the first time.

Charity was the first to speak. "I assume these abductions and murders occurred when Carmichael was stationed at these bases?"

"The one in Fort Sill, yeah," Chyrel replied. "And the one in Fort Bliss happened while he was on leave. Cruz had an apartment in a rundown complex in El Paso at the time. And Carmichael flew to Fort Bliss."

"So, she rounded up some women for the party?" Charity asked, sitting on the edge of the bed, crossing her legs. "Then Carmichael took leave to go down there to torture these women?"

"It fits the profile I'm putting together on both," Paul said, moving one side of the headphones up, leaving the other over his ear to hear whatever he was listening to. "Once Carmichael is apprehended, I feel certain that a psych eval is going to reveal severe anti-social personality disorder. Certainly Cruz will. She's the dangerous one."

"You mean they could claim insanity and walk, after being arrested?" I asked.

"Doubtful," Paul replied. "APD rarely has a clinical diagnosis. They know right from wrong, but lack any empathy for their victims—or anyone and anything else. Most start out in early adolescence, tormenting, and killing animals, even pets. But there could be several other mental disorders associated with these two, so an insanity defense could be mounted. But walk? No, they'll spend the rest of their lives locked away in prison or in psychiatric confinement."

"I'm no psychologist," Andrew said. "But those two seem pretty social for folks having an anti-social disorder."

"It's all a put-on," Paul explained. "A sociopath can be extremely outgoing and sociable. They use this trait to manipulate their victims. And everyone is a potential victim. Sociopaths have a persistent and pervasive disregard for social norms and the rights and feelings of others. As Jesse would say, their moral compass is off by more than a few degrees. Nearly all serial killers show signs of sociopathy." Turning suddenly, Paul pulled the other ear-

shoes. In fact, I hadn't seen Charity with shoes on since she arrived.

She continued past the elevator and I yelled after her, "Where you going? The elevator's right here."

"The stairs," she called back over her shoulder.

Paul's voice came over the comm. "Good idea. Take the stairs. These people are swingers. Remember, you want them to think you're one of them."

"I don't think they've been called swingers since probably the nineties," Charity said.

"We're on the ninth damned floor," I muttered, sprinting after Charity. "If not swingers, what are they?"

She pulled the heavy steel fire door open and disappeared. I yanked it open and started down the concrete-and-steel steps after her.

"I've heard it called *the lifestyle*," Charity's voice echoed from below.

I could hear her breathing hard now, as I vaulted to the next floor's landing to catch up. Hearing her labored breathing, and knowing that I was keeping pace with a former Olympian, fifteen years younger than me, made me feel quite pleased.

Pausing to compose ourselves at the door to the first-floor lobby, Charity turned toward me. Her breathing was a bit more labored than my own.

She looked me up and down, smiled and winked. "Not bad, for an old-timer. We should, uh...*work out* together again."

If my face hadn't already been flushed beet red, it was now. Doing pushups, face-to-face with a beautiful woman in a bikini will cause all kinds of thoughts to enter a man's head.

Smiling broadly, knowing she'd caught me in a mental act of debauchery, Charity stepped past me, her breasts gently brushing my arm, and pushed the door open. We walked casually through the lobby and into the bar, carrying our beach towels.

The lounge was empty, save for the bartender, who rose from his stool and put his paper aside. I ordered two Cokes on ice and he poured them quickly.

"You still have an open tab, Mister Buchannan."

Remembering his name, I said, "Sorry, Nick, I don't have my wallet on me. Can you add these to the tab?"

"You can charge it to your room, if you'd like."

"Thanks," I said. "We're in nine-fifteen."

He glanced quickly at Charity, and one corner of his mouth turned up slightly as he produced the register's printout and a pen. I added a generous tip, signed it, and slid it back to him.

We carried our drinks to the door and paused. Carmichael and Cruz were at their usual table. "Ready?" Charity asked.

I nodded and she pushed through the door, stepping out into the sunlight. Outside, she paused and handed me her drink while she removed the yellow beach wrap and draped it over her arm. The sun, now halfway to the western horizon, coupled with the stark whiteness of her bikini, made Charity's exposed skin glow like that of a bronze goddess. I was reminded again of her lack of tan lines.

Taking her drink back, she sipped slowly from the straw as she casually turned her whole body, shadows falling across every curve. Pulling Chyrel's big white sunglasses low on her nose, Charity surveyed the patio area.

the forward area unfinished. Hell, I could drag a couple of king-sized mattresses in there."

"Wait," Penny said. "What about Diane and whatshis-name?"

"Cliff," Jenna added. "Yeah, he has to work on Friday. We can't leave early."

"Screw 'em," Carmichael said. "Seven is more than enough."

Jenna pulled her sunglasses down. Her eyes were pale blue, like sea ice, or the eyes of a Siberian tiger. But, like Penny's, they had a slight dull haze. "You two and five women? Do you really think you guys have that kind of stamina?"

Carmichael sat back in his chair, as the bartender placed drinks from a tray on the table. "If we don't," he said with a lecherous smile, "we can just sit back and watch you girls for a while."

Taking a sip from my drink, I could tell the bartender remembered me from before. The drink was more rum than Coke. I lifted my glass and nodded at him.

"Whatta ya say, Stretch?" Cruz asked, trying to look seductive, leaning against Penny, and pulling her close. "If we can move up the departure to Friday morning, do you think you can convince Ginger and Gabby to come?"

My phone vibrated against my leg startling me. I took it out and saw that I had a text message from Devon. I grinned at Cruz. "Oh, they'll come," I replied. Then to Carmichael, I added, "Right now, I'm needed elsewhere."

Carmichael laughed as if that was the funniest thing he'd ever heard. "I bet you are, boyo," he said. "I'll get hold of Mistrall and tell him to get the VIP stateroom at least habitable for you by tomorrow evening and we'll sail Friday morning."

I nodded at him as I stood. "Call me tomorrow. Suite nine-fifteen."

Leaving them, I went inside the bar and stopped. While I watched them, I told Deuce I was turning the earwig off to call Devon.

"How did I know you'd call rather than text?" she said by way of hello.

"You know me well. What's up?"

"You're still in Miami?"

"Yeah, but I should be home Friday evening. Is Finn okay?"

"He's fine," she replied. "I've been sleeping in your big bed, and he sleeps on the floor next to me." There was a pause. "Is Charity still with you?"

I hated having lied to her about who Charity was. "Not at the moment," I replied. "She's joined Deuce's team, at least temporarily. I think it's a good thing."

"Me too," Devon said. "I like her. I don't know how or why, but I do. Will she be keeping her boat here at your island?"

"I doubt it," I said, finally seeing a way to steer the conversation away from any involvement between me and Charity. "That's not her boat, though. It belongs to her boyfriend. He's on her boat now, down in the islands. It's a long story."

"Well, I have all weekend for you and her to tell it to me."

Me and her, I thought. "Want me to pick you up at Rusty's on Friday?"

"No," she said. "I'll have Deputy Philips drop me off Friday morning, after my shift. I'm going back to days on Monday and the lieutenant is giving me Friday night off to make up for last Sunday. Just when I was getting used to it."

We said goodbye as I watched Penny rise from her chair. She wiggled her cutoffs down over her hips and strode toward the pool. The black bikini softened her somewhat angular curves. At the edge of the pool, she raised her arms and dove in.

A few minutes later, I swiped the room card in the door and stepped inside. Someone new was talking to Deuce and Chyrel, his back to me. He was a broad-shouldered black man, my height, head shaved, wearing an expensive looking gray sports jacket.

When the door closed behind me, the stranger didn't seem to notice the sound. When Deuce looked at me, the stranger turned and I saw his disfigured face. He had burn scars on the left side, his left ear almost completely gone, but I recognized him immediately.

"Tom?" I said, crossing the room toward him. "Tom Broderick? What? How?"

"Hi, Jesse," Tom said. "Been a while."

Tom Broderick had been my battalion CO when I retired from the Corps, almost ten years ago. We'd first met, years before that, when he'd been assigned as my rifle platoon commander, fresh out of Officer Candidate School in Quantico, and I was a rifle squad leader. Tom had been a good officer and an exceptional leader, always eager to learn from his non-coms, who'd been around longer. Last time I saw him, almost three years ago, he was a full-bird colonel and the battalion commanding officer.

Grabbing his extended hand, I pulled him in for a man-hug. "When did you get here? What are you doing here?"

CHAPTER FIFTEEN

It was a fool's mistake. Once we knew that we couldn't just break into Carmichael's boat at the yard to get the emeralds back, we'd failed to move to the next obvious scenario: getting inside the boat after it left.

"We could force him to move them somehow," Deuce said.

"Same problem," Tony interjected. "Where he moves them might be even more secure, and taking him down in public while he's moving them, could get innocent people hurt."

"We'll have to go on the boat with him," I said. "With waterborne backup."

"We need your boat, Jesse," Charity said. "We need the *Revenge*."

"It's getting late," I said. "It's over a hundred miles, probably four hours running time in the dark. I can get down there in the plane before the sun goes down, and be back here about midnight."

"You'll have to stay," Chyrel said. "There's a chance you might be seen coming or going. Or, he might get bold and knock on the door, inviting you to dinner."

"Tony and Andrew, then," I said. "But driving down, then taking Rusty's boat up to my island; they might not get here until dawn."

"We'll have to work in shifts, anyway," Paul said. "Someone will need to monitor the bug in their room. I can bounce it to Tony and Andrew's comms, via the boat's internet."

"You can?" I asked. "I mean, I know Chyrel can."

"Yeah, he can," Chyrel said. "He's a fast learner. We'll take the first shift here, taking turns on the headphones. Then I'll switch it over to Tony and Andrew's headsets and they can take turns by just switching them off and on."

"Where are you staying, Tom?' Deuce asked, getting his attention first.

"Nowhere. I came straight here from the airport, and left my seabag in a locker there."

"I have a spare room," Paul offered. "Just twenty minutes from here. We can swing by the airport and grab your bag on the way."

"It's settled, then," Deuce said. "I'm going home, and Julie and I will both be back about sunrise. She can help from the van when the boats leave."

"I don't know if that's a good idea," I cautioned. "She's what? Six months pregnant?"

"Julie's gonna have a baby?" Charity cried out. Then she punched me on the shoulder. "Why haven't you told me this." She went straight to Deuce and hugged him tightly around the neck. "Congratulations, boss!"

While they talked excitedly, I pulled Tom aside. "Once this is done, you're welcome to stay with me. I have a little island in the Middle Keys, with two bunkhouses that get little use."

"Don't let him fool you," Tony said, getting Tom's attention first. "His *little island* is a paradise, Colonel. Welcome aboard."

"Just call me Tom, okay?" Then to me he added, "That sounds good, at least until I get on my feet. I think I'd like to be close to the office, though."

"Open ended," I said. "Some of these folks have lived there for weeks at a time. There's plenty of room."

Handing Andrew the keys to the house, and my debit card for fuel, I said, "Use it as a credit card. I'll let Rusty know you're on the way and will need his skiff. It'll be dark when you get to the island, and Finn's there alone at night. I'd appreciate it if you brought him with you. Stay to Harbor Channel and East Bahia Honda Channel to the Seven Mile Bridge. Once you're in open water, you can run full speed all the way to Biscayne Bay. There's a marina just across Bayside from here called Prime Marina Miami. The coordinates are on the *Revenge's* chart plotter. I'll call them and arrange a slip. Fuel up when you get there. Just remember—"

"If I break it," he interrupted, "I bought it."

"Be careful," I said. "When you get there Finn will probably be alone, and I don't know how he'll react."

I wasn't concerned that they'd have any trouble with the *Revenge*. Both men were very familiar with the boat and had tons of offshore and nearshore experience.

The two men left, and Paul and Deuce were right behind them, taking Tom along. When I turned around, I suddenly realized it was just me and the two women. Charity was sitting on one bed and Chyrel, the other.

"I don't know about y'all," Chyrel said, "but I'm about nine ways to hungry. Does this place have room service?"

"I have a better idea," I offered. "There's a restaurant across the street, next to the grocery store. They order crawfish and tilapia from Carl. It's called Monty's Raw Bar. Care to try it out?"

"Sure," Chyrel said, grabbing her go-bag and heading toward the bathroom, "but I need to change. Besides, hungry or not, we'll have to wait here at least an hour before we go anywhere."

"Why do we need to wait?" I asked.

"Because," Charity said, flopping back on the bed, hands behind her head, "it'd take you at least that long to satisfy two women that are *hotter than a pair of two-dollar pistols*."

As the door to the bathroom closed, I heard Chyrel laughing uncontrollably. Charity rolled over on her side and started to laugh, too.

An hour later, we crossed the street and walked to the restaurant, just around the corner. We didn't see Carmichael or Cruz or anyone else for that matter.

"I'm just saying," I said, opening the door to the restaurant. "We can make other arrangements."

"Don't be stupid," Chyrel said. "We're all adults here. Yeah, we're playing some kinda cat-and-mouse game with these people, and I know you'd prefer to just bash his skull in, but we have to do it with finesse. That means putting on the illusion that we're a threesome."

Charity walked through the door, followed by Chyrel. "I get it, but did you both have to grab my butt in the lobby? There wasn't anyone around."

"Just practicing," Chyrel said.

Charity stopped just inside the door and turned toward me. "Don't look now, but the rat and his mice are here. Three o'clock, just around the corner."

The hostess was at a little kiosk just ahead, with dining areas off to both sides, and an open-air dining area on a large palm thatch covered deck off the back.

"I don't give a shit," I said. "I'm hungry."

The two of them quickly fell into character as they followed me.

"Dinner for three?" the young lady at the kiosk asked.

"Outside, if possible," Charity said.

"Stretch!" I heard Carmichael shout. I rolled my eyes as I turned toward them, then smiled, and waved. He motioned us over.

"Do it," Charity said, nudging me.

"Thanks," I told the hostess. "We're going to join our friends."

Together, the three of us walked toward Carmichael's table. Cruz, Penny, and Jenna were with him, along with another man. He was younger, non-threatening looking. Probably a friend of either Penny or Jenna. As we approached, the other man suddenly stood.

"Yeah, I get it now," he said. His eyes flashing toward us. "Two is better than one." He looked back at Carmichael, obviously angry. "Fuck you, man!"

We stepped aside, as the young man stormed past. "Don't pay him any mind," Carmichael said, waving us forward. "Sit down. It's great that you showed up here. Now we can get to know each other."

"Who was that?" I asked, pulling out two chairs for Chyrel and Charity. Carmichael had his back to the wall, Cruz on one side and the two girls on the other.

"That was Cliff," Jenna said. "Wilson just told him that we're leaving Friday morning, instead of in a week."

"He didn't seem to be taking the news well," Chyrel said.

"He has a job," Penny said. "And he'd arranged to have a week off, but not next week. The week after. And now it's too late to change it with his boss. I'm Penny."

I introduced Chyrel and Charity to everyone, using their aliases. "You know what boss spelled backward is?" I asked Penny. "A double SOB."

The sophomoric joke didn't seem to register for a minute, and then she smiled. "Oh, I get it."

"So, what'd the boatyard say?" I asked Carmichael, as I sat down between Chyrel and Charity.

Carmichael went on to tell me that Mistrall wasn't happy about rescheduling the larger part of the work, but understood. "By now, they probably have the bulk of the VIP cabin done. That's what I'm gonna call it, the VIP cabin. Another guy is gonna run the wiring and plumbing in the forward section tonight, then they'll lay decking and build a partition around the head tomorrow. He's even got three super-king mattresses, he's gonna install, one forward and two side-by-side just aft of that one."

"Sounds cozy," Charity said, smiling at Cruz.

The waitress arrived with our drinks. Before anyone could even look at the menu, Carmichael said, "We need some oysters. A whole lot of oysters."

Cruz laughingly agreed, and Carmichael told the waitress to start steaming and bring them out two dozen at a time.

"Oysters are good for the libido," Jenna said.

When we left the restaurant an hour later, Chyrel said, "I need another shower."

"Yeah, me too," Charity agreed. "I mean, I've been with another woman before, and enjoyed it. But the things they were talking about? And over dinner?"

"These are some perverted individuals," I said. "Another day and a half, then we can turn the lot of them over to the cops."

"How do girls that young get roped into stuff like that?" Charity asked. "Never mind. Obviously, they meet people like Cruz and Carmichael."

Reaching the room, I opened the door and we went inside. I pulled a quarter from my pocket and told Chyrel to call it.

"Heads," she said. "What are we flipping for?"

It landed on the bed, tails up. "Charity gets the first shower," I said.

I caught Charity's not-so-subtle wink at Chyrel. "The shower's big enough for all three of us."

"Yeah, Jesse," Chyrel said. "Gotta keep up appearances."

"Get in there," I told Charity, spinning her gently toward the bathroom, hoping they were both joking. "And be quick about it."

Chyrel sat at her computer and turned on the bug in Carmichael's room. They'd stayed behind to have a few drinks when we left. Picking up a small desk mic, she spoke into it. "Andrew, I got the sound on here. How are things going there?"

"Haven't heard anything over the comm," Andrew's voice said over the laptop's speakers. "Finn was a little defensive at first and it took a while to get the *Revenge* past the sailboat, but we're heading toward the lighthouse in Harbor Channel now."

"Damn," I muttered, taking a pillow from each bed, and tossing them on a recliner. "I forgot about that. Ask him if Finn's okay."

She relayed the question and he replied that Finn was aboard, napping already, and that Tony had gone below and was going to set up the pull-out sofa to use as a watch bunk, as soon as he made some coffee. "We can take turns getting a little sleep on the way."

"Sounds good," Chyrel replied, as I heard the water turn off in the bathroom. "We'll have the comm until about midnight, then I'll switch it over to you guys. Remember to turn it off when you go to sleep."

Charity came out of the bathroom, a towel wrapped around her hair and another around her body. I didn't say anything, just stepped past her into the bathroom and grabbed a spare blanket off the shelf in the linen closet.

"What are you doing with that?" Charity asked, slipping past me again after retrieving her go-bag.

"You two can have the beds," I said. "I'll sleep on the recliner."

"Don't be silly," Chyrel said, following Charity into the bathroom with her bag. "The beds are plenty big enough for two."

"Or three," Charity said, closing the door.

This is gonna be a long night, I thought, as I continued to make up the recliner. *Another long night.*

opportunity comes along. In the modern human species, the opportunity is all around, yet the taking at will is done only by lowlife turd fondlers, like Carmichael.

I grinned at myself in the mirror, remembering Charity had said she liked that term.

In today's modern society, there's usually a courtship, and traditionally the man takes the lead. It's been the same for generations of humans, the man asking the woman for a date, holding the door, paying for the meal, and making the first move. Many feminists disapprove of these things, saying they're demeaning, and that women should open their own doors, and not be afraid to take the tradition-ally male role of being the aggressor in a possible relation-ship, asking the man out if she likes him.

I've met a few women like that. Devon was sort of that way. She'd definitely made the first advance, and damned near destroyed me the first time we'd slept together. But it never really felt like she was being overly aggressive. Some women have learned to take what *they* want, and still make the man feel like he was the triumphant sexual aggressor. My views might be considered old-fashioned, but I was raised by my grandparents.

My shower lasted only a few minutes. Without the need to shave, the seven minutes I once spent had dwindled to just five. I turned the light off before exiting the bath-room, not wanting to disturb the two women. I needn't have bothered. They were sitting up, talking.

Another sound came from over on the desk. When I walked over toward it and dropped my bag, I realized the sound was coming from the computer. The sound of people having sex. More than two people.

I quickly located the *volume down* button and held it until the sound disappeared. "I'm sorry," I said, without knowing why. "You don't need to hear this."

"It's just two people making the beast with two backs," Chyrel said. I could feel her grin, even with my back to her.

"And someone else smacking his ass to make him go faster," Charity added.

"We should leave it on," Chyrel said. "They may slip and say something we can use."

"And just what do you mean, *we don't need to hear this?*" Charity asked. "We, as in women? It's mostly the two women making the noises. All he's doing is grunting like a rutting ape. It's not like we haven't heard it before."

In the battle of the sexes, men are at a distinct disadvantage at times, and I knew when to give up the skirmish. I was a dinosaur in today's battle, just as I am against our current enemy. I was old.

Grabbing my money clip and wallet, I said, "Fine, listen all you want. I'm gonna go get a drink. Maybe two."

I turned the volume up on the computer and headed for the door. There was no way I was going to listen to two women having sex with one man *and each other*, while trapped in a room with these two.

"Hand the comm over to Andrew at midnight," I said, closing the door behind me. As I walked past Carmichael's room, I heard a sharp smack and Carmichael grunted.

Am I a prude? I asked myself. Two loving parents raised me until I was eight. They had a normal relationship and I don't think either of them ever even looked at someone of the opposite sex, at least not in that way. They never invited another person into their bed, and their bedroom door was closed when they slept. The grown-up me knew that they made love, probably every night they were together. They were young, married, and devoted to each other.

After my parents died, I went to live with Mam and Pap. At the time, they'd been younger than I am now. They held hands in public, but I don't recall ever seeing them kiss. I'm sure they did, of course; and they had an active sex life, I suppose. But it was one man and one woman, behind closed doors.

If that's prudish, I'm a prude.

Charity had said more than once that she enjoyed sex with both men and women, and it sure didn't seem like Chyrel was acting when they kissed out by the pool. Charity had even said that Devon was bisexual. There were a lot of things I just didn't understand and probably never would. What people did in the privacy of their bedrooms, I'd always considered was their own business, definitely none of mine. If they identified themselves as gay, lesbian, or somewhere in between, who was I to say otherwise?

Getting off the elevator, I found the lobby was nearly deserted. It was Wednesday, and it was late. Just a few miles north, in South Beach, that didn't matter much. But here in Coconut Grove it was time to roll up the sidewalks.

The lounge was nearly empty, just a waitress and bartender, talking at the end of the bar, and two couples at different tables. I went to the opposite end of the bar and took a stool next to Tony's potted palm.

"Get ya something?" the bartender asked, walking casually toward me. It wasn't Nick, nor the guy who was working the other night.

"Do you have any good rum?" I asked, leaning my arms on the bar. "Something dark, but not some self-proclaimed captain?"

His eyes fell to the tattoo on my forearm. "Recon, huh? Pusser's good for you?"

"Perfect," I replied. "Make it a double; chilled."

"Name's Mike," he said, scooping ice into a shaker. He reached under the bar without looking and produced a bottle of dark rum with a red label, and pulled the cork with a satisfying pop. I recognized it as the fifteen-year-old aged rum from Pusser's.

"Call me Stretch," I said.

He poured without measuring, then capped the shaker and swirled it around with some ice cubes a few times, before pouring it through the strainer into a highball glass.

"Nice to meet you, Stretch," Mike said, placing the drink in front of me. "My brother was a Recon Marine. First one's on the house."

"Thanks," I said. "Your brother get out, or retire?"

"Killed in action in Fallujah."

"Sorry for your loss," I said, raising my glass, "but grateful for his service."

"Thanks," he said. "You serve in Vietnam?"

I nearly choked on my first sip. And with good fifteen-year-old rum, that's practically a sacrilege. "Um, no," I replied. "That was over before I enlisted."

Do I look that old? I wondered. Saigon fell when I was in junior high school. I'd just turned fourteen, but had already made up my mind to follow my father and grandfather in becoming a Marine.

"Sorry," Mike said. "My dad was a Nam vet. Army, though. When were you in?"

"Enlisted in seventy-nine and retired in ninety-nine."

He considered it a moment, I could see in his eyes that he was thinking back to events in his own life during that time. It's how people remember when things happened. Unlikely that he'd remember the former; he couldn't have been more than twenty-five or so.

"Peacetime Marine, huh?"

A common enough misconception. People remember the big wars and consider the time between Vietnam and Iraq, the whole last quarter of the previous century and two years into the next, as all peaceful. The world was far from a peaceful place during that time, and I knew it personally, but let it slide. "Yeah, for the most part."

"So, what brings you to Miami, Stretch? I'm guessing business. You already have the tan."

"It's all pleasure," I heard Charity say behind me. Turning, I saw that she'd changed into tight black jeans and a red tank top, scooped very low in front. And she was wearing shoes, which as far as I could remember was the first time since her arrival. Heeled sandals, but shoes, nonetheless.

"You ready to go, baby?" Chyrel asked from my other side. She'd changed also. Tight white pants and a blue and yellow silky-looking blouse.

"What're y'all doing?" I asked, as Mike retreated to the other end of the bar, grinning.

"Look," Charity whispered, her breath warm against my ear. "We're sorry for teasing you."

"And want to make it up to you," Chyrel added, whispering in my other ear.

Charity pulled on my arm. "While we show you at the same time, that men and women can have fun, even flirt, and just be friends. There doesn't always have to be benefits."

"Come on, Jesse," Chyrel said. "Let's blow this place and go have some fun. Andrew and Tony have things covered until morning, and there's nothing for us to do until then anyway."

"Where are we going?" I asked, tossing down the rum, leaving a ten on the barn, then standing and allowing myself to be led along.

"South Beach," they both replied in unison.

CHAPTER SIXTEEN

Waking the next morning, my head hurt. Not a full-blown, brain-crushing hangover. More of a low throb, requiring copious amounts of coffee. I could see through the sliding glass door that it was beginning to get light outside. The drapes were wide open.

Turning my head, I saw Chyrel and Charity lying in the other bed. Chyrel was on her back, legs tangled in the sheets. She was wearing only her bra and panties. Charity lay on her belly next to her, clothed only in black panties.

I shook my head, trying to clear the cobwebs brought on by too much alcohol and not enough sleep. That turned the pain up a notch.

We'd hit a number of night clubs, drinking and dancing. I'd eventually relaxed and had fun. Real fun, like I'd never experienced before. But I knew nothing had happened between any of us, aside from a lot of toying remarks and touches.

I heard a chirping noise from beside the bed, and recognized it as a message alert. Throwing off the covers, I realized I was wearing only my skivvies. That had been Chyrel's idea. To sit across from one another and talk, wearing only our underwear. Charity wasn't wearing a bra under her tank, and had no problem stripping down to her underwear and acting as if it was the most normal thing in the world.

I grabbed my cargo shorts from the floor and pulled them on, taking my phone from the pocket.

It was a message from Andrew, time stamped just two minutes before. They were on their way over from the marina, after walking Finn and locking him up in the salon.

"Get up!" I said, urgently.

The two women started to stir, and Charity rolled over. Absolutely no tan line, whatsoever.

"Charity!" I said louder. "Chyrel, get up and get dressed. Andrew and Tony will be here any minute."

Charity was on her feet instantly, crouched between the beds, fists up and clenched, and fully alert.

I turned my back. "Will you two hurry up and get dressed? The others are on their way up here right now."

Finding my shirt from the night before, where I'd tossed it toward a chair but missed, I snatched it up and pulled it over my head. I tore into the coffee cart, looking for just a plain old brew, as the two women scurried to cover themselves.

While I was setting up the coffee maker, a knock came at the door. Chyrel and Charity scrambled to get their belongings together before disappearing into the head. The door opened before I got to it, and Tony came in.

He looked up, as he entered the room. "Morning, Jesse," he said, as he handed me a thermos.

I opened it and smelled. "Thanks, Tony. This hotel doesn't have much in the way of coffee."

"Have a good night?" Andrew asked following him in.

"What makes you ask?" I said defensively, as I ripped open the plastic on two paper cups. I filled them, plus the cup on the thermos and two porcelain mugs.

Tony stopped in the middle of the room, surveying the scene. Aside from both beds looking like a wrestling match had occurred, nothing was out of place. I usually sleep very light, with only the spot I lay on becoming disturbed, but last night I hadn't slept all that well. We'd returned to the room after three, just a little buzzed on liquor. During our nearly naked group chat, I'd brought up the subject of Charity's boat. Chyrel offered to help, and we'd talked about the subject while Chyrel snooped.

Chyrel had been the one to bring up the incident where Stockwell had given Deuce the electronic equipment. After searching through a number of government computers and not finding anything on Charity's boat, she'd searched the database on registered vessels.

That was where she'd found *Wind Dancer*, by the registration number. She matched it to the hull number from when the boat was built over seventy-five years ago. Both showed the current owner to be Charity Styles.

"It's your boat," Chyrel had told her, excitedly. "In every single way. It's yours."

Charity had asked her if she was sure, and Chyrel smiled. During the whole conversation, they'd been dressed just as they'd been when they woke up. It was then that Chyrel told her that the same applied to a helicopter in Puerto Rico.

She'd gone on to explain that according to every document and registration she could find on any database,

Charity owned both the sailboat and helicopter, and had for several years.

Chyrel finally stepped out of the bathroom. She was dressed in her usual attire: baggy jeans and a loose-fitting, long-sleeved blue blouse.

"I'll make our bed," Chyrel said to Charity dropping her bag on the floor at the foot of it. "You can make Jesse's, while the guys fill us in. Hey, Tony. Hey, Andrew."

Charity exited the bathroom, also dressed comfortably. In her case, bare feet, and boat clothes.

"Hi, girls," Tony said. Andrew only nodded, while he too looked around the room.

"Yeah," I replied to Andrew, handing him a mug of coffee. "I slept okay. Did Carmichael and Cruz say anything after we switched the comm over?"

"A lot of *yes, yes, yes*," Andrew said. "But nothing noteworthy."

"There were a couple of *oh my gods* thrown in toward the end," Tony added.

"Uncomfortable to listen to, yeah," Chyrel said, completely back to her usual persona, a far cry from the woman who was grinding against both me and Charity last night on the dance floor. "But it's necessary. Did they say anything at all useful?"

"No," Tony said, clearing his throat. "Basically, they just rolled over and passed out about three hours ago."

"Good," I said. "That means they won't be awake for several more hours."

Chyrel finished the bed and sat at her computer, giving me a sly wink, before striking a few keys on the keyboard. A distorted sound came from the speakers.

"Snoring," Charity said. "Not sure if it's him or one of the hers."

"Anyone else hungry?" Tony asked.

"I could eat," Chyrel said, turning in her chair. "Just in case, we shouldn't go down together. I hacked into the hotel security system and have the video feed of the hall camera, and the feed from the bug, both forwarded to my phone. I can listen inside and watch their door from anywhere."

"I'm starved," I said. "You guys go down to the restaurant and get a table with an adjoining empty table and the three of us will be right behind you."

Tony and Andrew left, carrying hotel coffee mugs with them.

"About last night," I said, closing the door and turning toward the two women.

"Nothing happened," Charity said. "We had some fun, let our hair down, and raised the roof in a few places."

"Raised the roof would be an understatement."

"It was all in fun, Jesse," Chyrel said. "You needed it, Charity needed it, and I damned sure needed it."

"It *was* fun," I said. "And completely innocent. Y'all made some of those bar patrons think I was some sort of famous movie star or something." I sat on the corner of my bed, getting a disapproving look from Chyrel. I stood back up and grinned. "And you probably made a bunch of men hornier than hell. Maybe even a few women."

"Including you?" Charity asked, putting a hand on my forearm. Her touch was like fire.

"Sorry, one last jab," Charity said. "Let's go eat breakfast, then figure out what our next step should be."

When we arrived in the restaurant there was a buffet, and Tony and Andrew were already digging in. They sat at a corner table with an empty table next to them. Both men were seated with their backs to the walls.

We sat down and a waiter arrived, asking if we wanted coffee. I told him to bring a pot and we'd hit the buffet. Once we were again seated, I said, "I want to go to the boatyard and see if I can get aboard. Tell the owner that I forgot something."

"Think he'll remember you?" Tony asked, wiping his mouth with a napkin.

"Probably," I replied. "The chest isn't large, I'm sure I can fit all the stones in my cargo pockets, or just put the chest in a pillowcase and stuff it with dirty linen. Carmichael won't be up for hours yet."

"And if he doesn't let you" Andrew asked. "What if he calls Carmichael?"

"We can burn that bridge when we get to it," I replied. "I think it's worth a shot."

"Maybe instead of you forgot something," Charity said, "tell the man that you want to put something on the boat. Sort of a bon voyage gift or something."

"Good idea," Andrew said, trying, and failing at a whisper. "Something he wouldn't likely call Carmichael about. But what?"

"Something the boatyard owner would understand," Charity said. "Maybe a Saint Brendan statue? He's the patron saint of sailors."

"Yeah, where you gonna find that?" Tony asked.

"You'd be surprised how commercial Catholicism has become, Tony," Charity said, then turned to me. "There was a store just outside the airport, Botanica Nena. They'll have them."

"Okay," I said, "I'll go with Tony and Andrew. If I succeed in getting aboard and finding the emeralds, we'll head straight to the *Revenge*. You two stay here and keep an eye on our friends."

"And if you can't get aboard?" Chyrel asked as my phone vibrated in my pocket.

Taking it out, I saw that I had a text message from Deuce. "That's Deuce," I said. "He, Julie, and Paul are in the van, parked across the street again."

"Where's your friend Tom?" Chyrel asked.

"He doesn't say," I replied. "If I can't get aboard, I'll come back here and we'll proceed with the original plan: wait until we're on the water, then overpower Carmichael."

Hitting the call button, I waited for Deuce to answer. When he did, I told him about our plan and asked about Tom.

"He has a line on a condo," Deuce said. "It won't be available for two weeks, but he wanted to see it. It's on Lower Matecumbe Key about fifteen miles from the office. He sounded pretty excited about it. Look, if the boatyard owner resists even a little bit, I want you to just leave the gift with him and ask him to put it aboard before launching."

"Will do," I said, ending the call.

We ate quickly, then the women went back up to the room and I walked out to the parking lot with Tony and Andrew.

"So," Tony said, as we approached my rental car, "Who slept with who last night?"

I pulled my sunglasses down slightly and glared at him over the roof of the car.

"Easy, big guy," Tony said raising both hands, as if in surrender. "A joke. Everyone knows you're too much of a wet blanket. Say, where'd that saying come from anyway?"

Grinning, I pushed my shades back up and opened the door. "A person who puts out fires."

We found the store easily enough, and they did indeed have a statue of Saint Brendan, an Irish saint also known as *The Navigator* or *Anchorite*. Being Irish, I probably should have known that, but I didn't.

Just as we pulled into Mistrall's parking lot, all three of our phones began chirping. Mine was a text from Julie telling me to turn on my earwig. All three of us started digging into pockets, apparently having received the same message.

Turning it on, I stuck the comm in my ear. "What's up, Jules?"

"Are Tony and Andrew with you?" she said, without greeting.

"We're here," both said at once.

"Your guy just woke up. He got a phone call; apparently, the boatyard is finished and they're ready to put the boat in the water. He's on his way there now."

"Go!" Tony said. "Out of the lot and turn left. There's a strip mall next door with a big parking lot that has a view of the docks."

I reversed and followed Tony's directions. As I pulled into the nearly empty lot, he directed me to the slight shade afforded by a tired-looking willow tree.

"There he is." Tony said, just as I buzzed the windows down and shut off the engine.

A cab was turning into the parking lot we'd just left. When it stopped, the passenger door opened and Carmichael got out. He was alone. He paid the driver, said a few words to him, then disappeared inside the building.

A few minutes passed, then I heard a sound familiar in larger boatyards. "That's a travel lift starting up," I said. "They'll be putting the boat in the water soon."

After several more minutes, the boat hoist came into view, a giant gantry frame on wheels. The big trawler was hanging below it on four heavy straps. Slowly, the huge machine inched its way toward two narrow concrete piers, built just far enough apart that the lift could straddle the water between them.

"Call coming in on the house phone," Chyrel said. "Gimme a sec—there. Your phone should be ringing, Jesse."

The caller ID was blocked. I didn't know if it was because Chyrel hacked into the hotel's phone service, or the caller was blocking his identification. I answered it anyway.

"Stretch, it's Wilson. Hope I didn't wake you."

"No, we just got back to the room after breakfast."

"You, as in you and the missus, or all three of you?"

"What do you think, Wilson?"

He chuckled and said, "Hey, look. The boatyard finished the work early. They worked a double crew all night, and it's awesome."

"How soon before they can launch it?" I asked, watching the man at the helm. He was moving the trawler to the dock as the travel lift backed away.

"She's in the water now. You guys want to move the departure up? I think we can be ready to leave in time for the high tide."

"Is that important?" I asked, playing dumb.

"Yeah, it'll shave quite a few hours off the crossing. If we can go down to the southern end of Biscayne Bay, versus going north and through the main shipping channel."

This made no sense. The Port of Miami shipping channel was only a few miles to the north, and Cape Florida Channel was just a few miles south. Both had at least twenty feet of water. There was no need to go ten miles down to the narrow cuts through the shoal waters at the Safety Valve.

"What time do you think we should leave?"

"It's about two hours down to Soldier Key," he replied. "If we get there at slack tide, about two o'clock, we can ride right through."

"So you want to shove off at noon?"

"No later than that," Carmichael said. "If we get there too late, it could be a bumpy ride, with the outflow from the bay pushing us faster than we need to go in a narrow channel."

"Got it," I said. "The girls are getting ready to head down to the pool, let me talk to them and call you back. What's your number?"

"I'll call you back in ten minutes," he replied. "I have some things to attend to down below."

Telling him that was okay, I ended the call. "Is everyone on?" I asked.

"Paul's on the headset, monitoring the listening device in the room," Julie said. "When Carmichael left, the two women seemed to go back to sleep."

"We're both here," Chyrel said. "Twiddling our thumbs."

"What do you guys think?" I asked. "We have three hours. Should we go with his moving the schedule up?"

"We topped the tanks on the *Revenge* before docking," Andrew said. "She's ready to go."

"I don't know," Deuce said. "Why does he want to go all the way down to Soldier Key?"

"Yeah, I wondered that, too," I said, watching as Carmichael paced the deck of the boat. "Bimini's the natural choice for entry to the Bahamas, and it's due east of Miami. Going ten miles south only adds ten miles to the total trip."

"Maybe he just wants to start further south so he doesn't have to angle his way across the Stream," Julie said. "That's what Dad used to do all the time."

"Could be," Deuce said. "A slow trawler will get pushed a lot further north in the Gulf Stream's current. We just don't know everything they have planned."

"One thing's for sure," Chyrel said. "Jesse being the only other man on the boat, Carmichael's going to want to kill him soon after leaving Biscayne Bay, probably when we're in the Gulf Stream."

"Yeah," Andrew grunted. "If anything's left of the body, it wouldn't wash ashore until reaching the white cliffs of Dover."

"His boat draws more water than the *Revenge*," I said. "Probably five or six feet."

Tony nodded in the back seat. "The *Revenge* draws what? Four feet when adrift, and maybe three at speed?"

"A little less," I said. "I agree with Chyrel, he won't do anything while we're in the bay. Too much chance someone will witness it. And if shore is still in sight, one of the captives might try to swim for it. So we want to make the takedown in the bay, when he's not prepared or distracted."

"What do you want to do?" Julie asked.

"Tony and Andrew will leave ahead of us," I replied. "Head offshore through Cape Florida Channel and watch from outside, pacing us in the bay. We'll have our earwigs on, and they'll be able to see us on radar. I'll try to get him to tell me which cut, and if he doesn't, the *Revenge* has the advantage of speed and draft. As he's navigating through the cut, bring her in fast. With luck, his boat will be beached in the shallows and, in the confusion, Charity and I can take care of the two of them."

"What about the other two?" Deuce asked.

"I think that, in the end, we'll find out that they're victims," Paul interjected. "Not complicit co-conspirators."

"That's the feeling I got," I added. "Chyrel can make sure the other two women stay out of the way."

Tony sat forward in the backseat. "If he searches you and finds guns, the jig's up."

"Same with communication," Charity said. "If the wind blows someone's hair, they could be seen."

I thought it over for a moment. "We'll have to go in unarmed and without the earwigs. We have plenty of bugs, I can put three under my shirt lapel and Paul can remotely activate one every hour as the batteries die. Plus we'll have our phones."

There was silence for a few seconds. Finally, Deuce said, "Going unarmed is a personal call for each of you."

"I'm in," Charity said, without hesitation.

"Chyrel," Andrew cautioned. "You're not a field agent."

"I can take care of myself," she replied. "I'm in."

Carmichael was looking at his phone. "Be ready to forward his call, Chyrel," I said.

"Coming in now," she said. "Transferring."

When my phone chirped, I tapped the *Accept* button. "Wilson?"

"Yeah," he replied. "What's the word? Are we leaving today, or hanging around the hotel tonight?"

CHAPTER SEVENTEEN

"I don't like moving things up," Deuce said, when we got in the van with the others, parked across from the hotel. Chyrel and Charity had joined them, as well.

Bending, I gave Julie a hug. Chyrel was sitting on a little folding stool next to her, with Paul crowded in on the other side, also on a stool.

"They're anxious," Andrew said from the front of the van, where he and Tony had moved to.

"But we're holding all the other cards," I said, pacing the floor in back. "We know they have the emeralds on the boat. We know what they plan to do with the three of us and the two girls. We know we have backup and a speed advantage. And we know they've done this before."

"What we don't know is the when, where, and how," Deuce said. "He could try to take you out with a gaff the minute you step on board."

"In the past," Paul said, lifting one earphone, "the bodies were found miles from where the abductions took place, and the dump sites all have two things in common. Each one was in an open area, miles from anything, where you could see in all directions for a considerable distance. And every victim was shot in the head, including the husband of the one married woman. They're careful, so I think that for where, it's safe to rule out the boatyard, or any place even remotely public. They're also habitual in how they murder, so a fish gaff is probably out, as well. They won't try to kill Jesse until they're at least in the middle of the bay, but I would say not until they're in international waters. And the idea of the Gulf Stream as a method of disposing of the body is very sound."

"Those cuts through the Safety Valve change all the time," Andrew said. "He'll need someone on the bow to help navigate."

"Don't forget," Chyrel said. "Jesse already told him that Charity was a boater, too."

Paul removed the headphones completely. "Carmichael is bound to know that Charity would be far less coopera-tive if Jesse is murdered," he said to Chyrel. Then, turning to the rest of us, he continued. "Cruz and the other woman in the room just left for the boatyard. I wasn't sure if the second woman was Penny or Jenna, until I saw them leave on the security camera. It was the blonde. I'm certain she, at least, is not in on Cruz's plan."

"He'll wait until we're in the Atlantic," I said. "I'm sure of it. We need to pack."

When we arrived at the boatyard a little after eleven, clouds were gathering far to the south. As the land temperature warms throughout the morning hours, it draws air upward, sucking in cool moist air from the ocean. When the two air masses collide, they create isolated thunderstorms common to south Florida this time of year.

Instead of going through the store, we followed a sign for the docks around the side of the building. I had a bunch of clothes stuffed into a backpack, which I'd gotten from the *Revenge*. On top of the clothes was a large cigar box, filled with a couple dozen hand-rolled Dominican cigars. Below the cigars was a false bottom, under which I'd stashed my Sig Sauer nine-millimeter handgun.

I also carried Chyrel and Charity's two large suitcases, as they preceded me toward the dock. Cruz was sitting on a boat box on the pier next to where Carmichael had docked the boat. Nobody else was in sight.

"Are we too early?" Charity asked, as she strode confidently toward Cruz.

"Early is good," the dark-haired woman replied. "Better to wait for the tide than to be late for the tide."

Penny came out of the aft salon hatch and saw us. "Wait till you see the playroom!"

"Playroom?" Chyrel asked.

"That's what Wilson calls it," Cruz said. "The whole front of the boat is full of mattresses."

Charity looked the smaller woman up and down, then did the same with Penny. "Sounds delightful," she said.

I knew the look was meant not only to incite Cruz's lust and make her feel that we were one of them, but that Charity was also examining both women closely for weapons, and estimating their abilities.

Charity had lived by her wits for the last eighteen months. She'd survived because she was not only tough and resilient, but smart and aware of her surroundings. I had no doubt that in some of the situations she'd been in, she'd been nice to everyone she'd encountered, but in the back of her mind, she'd been constantly developing and revising a plan to kill everyone in sight if it came to that. I knew, because it was what I would do, and was part of the solo infiltration techniques I'd taught Deuce's whole team over the last several years.

"Follow me, Stretch," Cruz said, mounting the boarding steps next to the boat. "Wilson and Jenna will be back shortly. He's inside taking care of business, and she's stuck in traffic."

Following Cruz into the salon, she turned and took one of the suitcases from me. "Wilson says to put your things in the VIP cabin."

I followed her through the salon and down the narrow steps to the forward berthing area. The workers had done a decent, though obviously rushed, job.

The sole had been finished and appeared to be mahogany, inlaid with another hardwood, maybe cherry. There was a section on the starboard side that was walled off, just aft the bow. It had a door, so I assumed it was the head Carmichael had mentioned.

But it was the beds that drew my eye. A wooden frame surrounded three large mattresses on the deck, holding them tightly together, in the shape of an L. Each was covered with light blue sheets. One mattress was in the bow, with room for the door to the head to open, and two aft the head, extending the full beam of the boat. You'd have to walk across a mattress to get to the head. All around the beds were large, dark blue pillows, leaning against the interior planking of the hull. It looked completely decadent, like the set of a cheap porn movie.

"Playroom, huh?" I teased.

"And am I looking forward to playing with you three," Cruz replied, leaning seductively against the stair rail. She was wearing the same black bikini top and cutoff jeans I'd seen her in before. Pushing away from the rail with her hip, she motioned me to follow as she stepped down into the lower cabin, and turned on a light.

I followed her down the steps. The deck here was the same mahogany-and-cherry sole as the bow area. A super-sized bed took up nearly the whole stateroom. It was built waist high against the starboard side, leaving only a few feet of room next to it, the whole length of the cabin. Under the bed were six large drawers, stacked two high. The bed was at least eight feet long and would easily sleep three people without touching one another. But I didn't think that was the intent. Like the playroom, it was done in light blue bedding, with dark blue pillows against the hull and both bulkheads.

A new ladder went up to a hatch in the overhead. Beyond the ladder, an enclosed area probably contained another head or a large storage closet.

"What's in there?" I asked, indicating the door with my chin.

"A really big shower. Room enough for four."

"That's it?" I asked, tossing one then the other suitcase on the bed, and shrugging out of the backpack.

"I'm sure it could fit more," she said, stepping closer. "It might be fun to see just how many."

Opening the pack, I took the cigar box out. One of Deuce's men on his old DHS team had been a retired FBI surveillance guy. He'd always said that hiding things in plain sight often worked better than the best of hiding places.

"Does Wilson allow smoking on board?" I asked, opening the box, and removing three cigars. I closed the box and put it in the top middle drawer below the bed.

"*Cubanos?*" she asked, taking one.

"Dominican," I replied. "Cuban cigars are illegal in the States."

"That is stupid on the part of the American government," Cruz said. "*Si*, smoking cigars is permitted on deck. *Anything* is permitted below deck."

Cruz stepped closer, not that there was a lot of room in the cabin to start with. I could feel the heat from her. She gave off a sexual vibe that was palpable and she was obviously ready, willing, and able.

"The forward bathroom has a handheld shower, a small sink, and a commode," she said. "There is a full-sized tub and shower in the aft cabin, plus a small day head next to the navigation desk. There is plenty of room and facilities for everyone."

She slowly eased past me, her nipples raking my belly like the tips of two knife blades. She fell against me for a moment as the boat rocked.

"The big shower," she said, looking up seductively, "is for when we just get too sweaty, and need to cool off together."

We returned to the cockpit and found Wilson and Jenna had returned. He was talking to the four women.

"Hiya, Stretch," the man said. "I was just explaining to the ladies what we all need to do to get safely underway. Since you have some boating experience, I'll need to count on you to help Rosana a little bit. Nothing major, just getting the boat untied and helping guide us through the channel later."

"Any way I can help," I replied. "Gotta say, I love what they did to the front part."

"Fo'c'sle," he corrected me. "Usually the crew quarters are in the front."

"Fossil?" I asked, dim-wittedly.

"No, it's pronounced foke-sul," he said, sounding out the word. Then turning to the four women, he showed off his maritime knowledge. "It's spelled like forecastle, but sailors shortened it to fo'c'sle. In old sailing times, the front of a ship, forward of the foremast, was built up real high, to give archers a place to shoot down on enemy vessels. The older crewmen, no longer agile enough to climb the rigging, lived in the cabins there, handling the foresails and anchors. It's where the term *before the mast* comes from, in saying how long a man has been a sailor."

"Just tell me what you need done," I said, as Wilson led the women to the boarding steps and waited until they boarded.

"Rosana, stand by the bow line," Carmichael said. "Stretch, go to the back of the boat and untie the line from the dock when I tell you to." He turned to the other women, leering at them. "The rest of you ladies, I had a big bench seat added forward. Go up there and look hot. Until further notice, the bikini is the uniform of the day, and once we're in international waters, that's totally optional."

Doing as I was ordered, I waited for him to climb up to the flybridge and start the engines. He spent a few minutes watching the gauges, and switching on the electronics. Finally, he yelled to Cruz to cast off the bow line. She tossed the line up onto the foredeck where Chyrel and Charity were now sitting with the two girls.

"Cast off the stern," Carmichael called down to me.

Quickly untying the line from the dock cleat, I saw Cruz standing by the rail amidships. She'd moved the boarding steps to the side, and stood ready to push the big boat away from the dock.

"Shove off," Carmichael ordered Cruz.

She pushed hard against the gunwale, her feet slipping on the dock. Slowly, the bow began to move out away from the dock. Why Carmichael hadn't used a spring line, or at least tractor steered with the throttles, I didn't know. But it was almost comical how hard the small woman was pushing, and how slowly the big boat responded to her effort.

Finally, with one last push, Cruz stepped across the gap onto the side deck and went forward. She started pulling up the large fenders, putting them in racks along the rail, and I did the same with the two alongside the cockpit.

Cruz continued forward and Carmichael called down for me to join him. I noticed that he waited until the boat had drifted in the direction he wanted to go, before he engaged the transmissions. The sound of water rushing from behind the boat by the twin props told me he'd shifted both to forward, instead of using them alternately to power the bow away from the dock.

Climbing the ladder to the flybridge, I went forward to where Carmichael sat behind the wheel.

"Have a seat, boyo," he said, leaning forward to look down at the foredeck. "Nothing much to do for the next couple of hours but enjoy the view."

Looking down over the low windshield, I saw Cruz wiggling out of her cutoffs to join the other four women on a wide, cushioned bench. It was built on the leading edge of the cabin roof and each of the five seats had a separate backrest that could be reclined almost flat. One by one, the women did just that: reclined to allow the full sun, and our eyes, to fall on their bodies.

"Yeah," Carmichael said, practically drooling. "Now there's a dream come true for any man."

"That's a heck of an idea," I said, sitting in one of the two matching seats on either side of his center seat. "Most boats like this don't have any forward seating, I noticed."

"So was yours," he said, with a grin. "Did ya see the ladder?" I nodded, as we idled slowly between the markers leading to deeper water. "I don't know why I didn't think of it myself," he continued. "When we're underway, the ladies can entertain themselves down there and you and I can tag team from up here."

I'd noticed when I was down in the cabin with Cruz that it had a locking hatch, made of sturdy hardwood, with substantial iron hinges and a locking mechanism that looked very secure. The lock required a key on either side. These two planned to keep their captives down there, safely locked away, until they'd used them up.

As Carmichael nudged the throttles up slightly, I saw *Gaspar's Revenge* passing by, out in the main channel of the Intracoastal. She was up on plane and heading south at about thirty knots.

"See that," Carmichael said, pointing at my boat. "Those clowns will burn more fuel in an hour than I will before morning."

"That's a deep-sea fishing boat, right?" I asked, again playing the land lubber, ignorant of all things nautical.

"Yeah," he replied. "See those long poles laying back on the roof? Those are outriggers, to hold the lines out away from the boat so they don't tangle."

"Never been deep-sea fishing," I said. "But if it's anything like bass fishing, I like to get to the good spots faster than the other guy."

"There's plenty of fish in the sea," he said, grinning like he'd told the world's greatest reverse pun.

I laughed anyway.

"Grab a couple of beers from that mini-fridge in front of you."

Opening the little built-in refrigerator, I saw that it was stocked with nothing but cheap beer and bottled water. The guy had millions in gems stashed just a few feet behind and below where we sat, but bought the cheapest beer they had at the marina.

I took two cans out and handed him one. "Just one or two, before we leave the bay," he said. "Don't want us to get all shit-faced before we navigate a narrow channel. We need to set up some ground rules."

"Ground rules for drinking beer or navigating channels?"

"Neither," he replied, leering over the windshield. "Ground rules for this floating orgy. Personally, I only like women, particularly women who also like women. Nothing personal, but I don't wanna see your junk. So we take turns, okay?"

"Take turns?" I asked, trying not to sound repulsed.

"I'm supplying three and you got two," he said, as if dividing up chips before a poker game. "We take turns with one, two, or all five at once. No pressure, though. The lifestyle rules hold on the water, too. If someone says no, or is uncomfortable, we back off."

"We're sort of new to the lifestyle," I said, removing the two cigars from my shirt pocket and extending one to Carmichael. "Care for one?"

"Thanks," he replied, taking it, and examining the odd chisel tip end to the roll.

From my pocket, I produced a folding knife and quickly poked a small hole near the tip of each cigar. "Keep the hole up," I said. "When you draw on it, the roof of your mouth will get the full flavor."

Lighting the cigar, Carmichael said, "Rosana chose you three, as well as Jenna and Penny. She goes both ways, and likes for me to watch her with other women. Your wife, her friend, and the two girls, are bi—or just straight-up lesbian, in Jenna's case. She hasn't let me touch her yet. Rosana's good with new girls, leading them slowly to where they want to go, but just don't know it yet. By the time we get back, your Ginger will be a full-on rock star when it comes to pleasing more than one person at the same time. And Jenna will be bouncing on top of both of us. But me? I only go one way."

Choking back the taste of the cheap beer, as well as the mental image of what he was talking about, I forced a grin and lifted my beer can. "Same goes with me."

Navigating the channel wasn't difficult. The engineers who'd dredged and drained the Everglades, straightened the Miami river and made it deep enough for small island freighters, and created waterfront property on a myriad of canals far inland, are the same ones who developed the waterfront. They drew a straight line on a chart from where they wanted to build to the nearest deep water, then dynamited the limestone bottom and brought in big dredging machines to dig the channel. In this case, it ran southeast in a perfectly straight line.

"What do you make of those clouds?" I asked, pointing toward the towering dark mass that was probably over Key Largo.

"Storms move west this time of year," he said. "By the time we get down to where we'll leave the bay those clouds will have rained out in the Everglades."

I wasn't so sure he knew the weather here as well as he thought. He was right about storms usually moving west this time of year, but they also tended to sprout up more storms around them, usually building to the north in the afternoon, each one marching ashore, creating a line of storms moving diagonally to the coast. Right now, the sky was clear and blue to the east; experience told me that could change quickly.

The old trawler took the wake from the *Revenge* while still several hundred yards from the last channel marker. The huge bow wave she creates had dissipated quite a bit, but the rollers still rocked the larger boat, splashing water from the port bow.

Reaching deep water at the end of the channel, Carmichael continued southeast, then made a wide turn into the main shipping channel, lining the slow-moving boat up with the red and green markers to stay in deeper water.

A sailboat passed, heading north under power. The three men in the cockpit stared, but I had no doubt that if they were asked five minutes later what color Carmichael's boat was, they wouldn't be able to say.

For the next half hour, we moved slowly south at six knots. Carmichael droned on monotonously about his boat, interjecting an occasional comment about the women.

The clouds ahead had darkened, and sheets of rain could be seen in two places slightly west of our course. I wasn't concerned with that storm; it was at least over Card Sound and moving west, well past where Carmichael had said he intended to cross into the Atlantic. But the wind was increasing, and far to the east, puffy white clouds had formed where earlier it had been clear blue sky.

The central bay was very wide, nearly eight miles. From our vantage point ten feet above the water, the shore was nearly out of sight. Staying to the shipping channel didn't really matter for a boat the size of Carmichael's trawler. Throughout most of the central bay, the water was at least ten feet, yet the man maintained the center line of the deeper shipping channel. Maybe an over-abundance of caution, but I was beginning to have serious doubts about the man's abilities outside of protected waters.

The *Revenge* had slowed, nearly a mile ahead of us. After a few minutes, I could tell by the absence of a bow wave that they had dropped to about the same speed we were going. I knew Andrew was at the helm and trusted him completely. After a few minutes, they turned southeast and disappeared through Biscayne Channel.

As we neared the channel, the wind was a steady fifteen knots, gusting to twenty or more. A small island freighter heading north out of the same channel had nearly all hands on the rail as we slowly cruised by. Again, I doubted if any of the men would remember seeing anything on this trip besides the five women stretched out side by side on the fore-deck. That would be something they'd talk about for years.

I suddenly had a new-found respect for the man if, in fact, Carmichael had intentionally sent them up to the bow as a diversionary tactic, so people wouldn't remember any details about the boat.

CHAPTER EIGHTEEN

Idling out of the marina, Andrew slowly brought *Gaspar's Revenge* up to her cruising speed of twenty-eight knots. He turned the expensive fishing machine into the main shipping channel, heading south into Biscayne Bay.

Back in the van with Julie, Paul had activated the first of four listening devices under the collar of Jesse's polo shirt, allowing Andrew, Tony, and Deuce to hear the conversation taking place on the fly bridge of Carmichael's boat.

After putting away the fenders and dock lines, Tony climbed up to the bridge deck, leaving Jesse's dog alone in the cockpit. He'd taken Finn for a long run around the marina, not just so the dog could relieve himself, but also to burn off energy for what could be a long boring day for him.

"He gonna be okay in the cockpit?" Deuce asked.

"Should be," Andrew replied. "He seems to prefer it."

"There they are," Tony said, pointing ahead and to starboard.

Carmichael's converted salvage vessel was in the middle of a side channel, moving slowly toward open water.

Deuce raised a pair of binoculars and studied the boat. He could see Jesse and Carmichael on the fly bridge. Both men were looking down at the foredeck. Moving the glasses lower, he saw Chyrel and Charity, along with Cruz and the two girls. Cruz was pulling her cutoffs down, and the other four women were getting comfortable on a wide bench on the front of the cabin roof.

"Do you suppose Carmichael has all of them up there for a reason?" Tony asked, also studying the other boat through binoculars.

Andrew looked toward the trawler. Even without binoculars, it was easy to spot the five women stretched out in the bright sunshine on the foredeck. "One thing's for sure," he said. "Any man who sees them probably won't remember any details about the boat."

"What's going on?" Julie's voice asked over Andrew's earwig.

Deuce lowered his binoculars. "All five women on board are sunning themselves on the foredeck," he told his wife. "Jesse and Carmichael are on the fly bridge."

"Sunning themselves?" she asked.

"In bikinis," Tony replied, still looking.

"Why?"

"That's what we were trying to figure out," Andrew said. "My guess is that it's an intentional move on Carmichael's part to divert any attention away from the boat and what it looks like."

"Activating the rooftop camera," Paul said. "I can control it from here so you guys can see it on the display there. Which direction is Carmichael's boat?"

"Three o'clock," Tony replied. "And falling astern."

Looking up, Andrew saw the closed-circuit monitor come to life. It began panning, moving from the scene directly in front of the *Revenge*, to what could be seen to starboard.

Finally, the trawler moved into the center of the picture, and Paul slowly zoomed in, as the *Revenge* powered through the light chop. The women were all seated now, legs stretched out on the deck and the backs of their chairs reclined.

Chyrel was on the port end of the bench, Charity right next to her. In the middle was the dark-haired Jenna, then Cruz, with Penny on the starboard end. Cruz was talking to Jenna, her hand on the younger woman's thigh.

Pulling back on the throttles, Andrew slowed the *Revenge*. "I don't want to get out of sight of them for any longer than we have to."

"The camera has image stabilization," Paul said. "I have it locked onto the trawler now. I sure wish I could hear what they're talking about up there on the front of the boat."

"Tom texted me just before we left," Deuce said, checking the radar. "I told him to go to where you are. But we'll be turning out of the bay shortly."

Andrew slowed the *Revenge* further, bringing it down off plane and matching the speed of the much slower trawler, which was nearly a mile behind them now.

They continued south, Deuce monitoring the camera feed as well as the radar. Biscayne Channel was a busy waterway, with commercial boats and yachts coming and going.

"A boat is coming into the channel," Deuce said to Andrew. "And there's a much larger one approaching the outer markers."

A moment later, a private sailing yacht could be seen beyond the tip of Cape Florida, moving toward the channel. Under power, it moved slowly through the deep channel and turned north toward the *Revenge*. A few minutes later, it passed by silently, one of the three men lounging in the cockpit raising a hand in a half-hearted wave.

"Tom's here, Andrew," Julie said. "Paul's showing him how to control the camera. Keep the *Revenge* as steady as possible, they're pretty far behind you guys."

Andrew glanced up at the TV monitor as the camera zoomed in on the five women.

"Chyrel and Charity are on the port side, right?" the new guy's voice asked over the comm.

"Yes," Paul replied. "Cruz is this one. She's one of the targets."

"She's telling the other dark-haired woman not to worry about something," Tom said. "She says that it will just be the two of them to start off, if that's what she wants."

"The other dark-haired girl we only know as Jenna," Julie said. "No hits on Chyrel's facial recognition program so far."

"Jenna is telling Cruz that she's fine with the others, but just isn't interested in the two men—um, is there something I don't know about here?"

"Jenna and Cruz are lesbian," Paul said. "Cruz tolerates men if she has to, but prefers sex with other women."

"Yeah," Tom said. "I guess that explains why Miss Cruz is massaging Jenna's thigh."

Julie went on to explain to Tom everything that was going on, and what they'd learned since yesterday. Tom interrupted on occasion, relaying what the women were talking about on the bow of the trawler, or asking pointed questions.

When the *Revenge* reached Biscayne Channel, Andrew bumped the throttles up and turned into it. Jesse and Carmichael were mostly talking about his boat, with Carmichael doing most of the talking. Occasionally, Tom interrupted the feed from the bug with something that Cruz was saying.

"Freighter inbound," Deuce warned, unnecessarily. Though much smaller than the big ocean crossing freighters, the island freighter still dwarfed the *Revenge*, and Andrew gave the larger ship a wide berth.

The freighter's crewmen must have all been in the pilothouse or below deck, because there wasn't a soul to be seen as the ship passed.

Andrew turned the *Revenge* into the ship's approaching wake. Though it was only moving at about four knots, the wake was large, nearly three feet. Whipped-up wind waves in the ocean were breaking across the shoals on either side, and the rushing tide coming in through the narrow channel made the whole area like the water in a washing machine, churning in many directions at once.

Confidently, Andrew turned back into the center of the channel and pushed the throttles up, bringing the boat up on plane to meet the churning water. He was confident not only in his own ability, but also in the boat he was handling. The *Revenge* knifed through it all with the ease of a much larger boat.

"Wind's increasing," Andrew said. "Looks like a storm is forming offshore."

"It's gonna be a rock and roll wait," Tony said, moving to the front of the cockpit, with a pair of binoculars. "Wind waves are building near shore, but the rollers don't look bad outside."

Pushing the throttles forward, Andrew said, "We'll get out beyond the chop, but I doubt we'll have a steady enough platform for Tom to see what's being discussed on the bow."

"It looks pretty rough in the bay south of here, too," Tony said. He sat at the starboard end of the forward bench, and looked out over Biscayne Bay. "High tide's in less than an hour, and waves are continuing into the bay after breaking over Safety Valve."

The skies to the east darkened quickly, as *Gaspar's Revenge* moved past the outer markers. Other cloud formations to the north and south looked like they could develop into storms as well. Andrew steered due east into the wind and oncoming waves, and straight toward the rising storm.

Occasionally, a wave would hit just as the bow was coming down off the last one, and the wide Carolina bow flares would shoot giant plumes of spray horizontally for ten yards or more. Andrew was always impressed with the dry ride of the boat, even in rough seas. With its modified vee hull and sharp entry, and having the bridge set well aft of amidships, the rough water was no match for the brute, and Andrew barely felt the impact of the waves.

On the sonar, the bottom slowly fell away past twenty feet, lessening the size and increasing the interval of the waves. Checking the chart plotter, Andrew saw that they were well out of the channel and nearing the three-mile limit. Pulling back on the throttles, he slowed the big boat until it dropped down into the choppy water.

"We'll hang out here," he said, keeping the bow into the wind and engaging the autopilot to maintain station.

The autopilot, using information from the GPS, sensed the push from the strong current and adjusted the heading. The boat turned slightly off the wind, which was doing a good job of holding their forward progress in check at idle and trying to push the boat back toward Biscayne Bay.

"That's them," Deuce said, pointing at an echo on the radar.

Tony stood up as the big boat wallowed slightly in the swells, and moved to the rail at the aft of the bridge deck. "Can't see them over the waves breaking on the shoal."

"We can on the camera feed," Julie said from inside the van. "It's on your roof, a couple of feet higher than you. But we're still losing it on occasion. Can you move closer?"

"Negative," Andrew replied, as a low rumble of thunder reached his ears. "We'd be too close to the shipping channel."

"I'm sure you already see them, Deuce," Paul said, "but I'm watching the weather radar forecast, and it's showing those storms east of you are going to intensify over the next hour and move into Biscayne Bay."

"Yeah," Deuce replied, watching the slow trawler on the radar. "The weather's gonna turn to shit out here, before they even get close to Soldier Key. Hopefully, Jesse can see this. That trawler's big and sturdy, but it's not built for a smooth ride in rough seas. They'll get hammered if they head out here."

Over the next thirty minutes, Andrew watched the radar and TV monitor, as the trawler continued south, and the autopilot did all it could to maintain the same position. Jesse had again asked Carmichael about the weather and he'd told Jesse not to worry about it, that his boat could handle anything.

"The boat might be able to handle it," Julie said, "but it just wouldn't be smart for him to continue with what he believes to be a novice crew."

"Looks like the women are moving off the bow," Tom said, just as a wall of light rain passed over the *Revenge*.

Over the bug on Jesse's collar, they all heard Carmichael shouting orders. Jesse asked him what he could do to help, and the man told him to check the straps on the dinghy. There was some scuffling and grunts, then Carmichael shouting to Cruz to take the lower helm, once she had everything secured. After a couple of seconds of silence, there were more scuffling noises, followed by a slight splashing sound.

Tony went quickly to the ladder, practically sliding down it on the handrails, as the rain began to pick up. Finn was jumping around on the deck, ready to play. The rain didn't seem to bother him, but Tony opened the door to the salon and put him inside anyway.

"Visual is gone," Deuce said, adjusting the rain clutter setting on the radar. "It's raining buckets out here."

Climbing back up to the bridge, Tony took his seat again on the port bench. Within minutes, all three men were drenched. Breaking out foul weather gear would just be a waste of time.

In the more than twenty years Andrew had served in the Coast Guard, he'd experienced a lot of rainy weather on the water, and more than his fair share of storms. To him and the two former SEALs, this was nothing. The bridge deck had side curtains, but the rain would probably be over before they could get the bridge buttoned up.

Then the rain began to fall harder.

"Losing them on radar," Deuce said, as the rain pounded on the fiberglass roof.

Everything on the bridge was waterproof, so the rain was little more than a minor distraction. Switching off the autopilot, Andrew turned the boat broadside to the five-foot swells and pushed the throttles forward. "Right before the rain hit us, it looked like it was a little clearer down to the south. I'm sure we'll pick them up again past Stiltsville."

"Stiltsville?" Paul asked over the comm.

"A bunch of stilt houses built out on Biscayne Flats during and after Prohibition," Julie said. "Some are in ruins, but I think one or two are still habitable."

Andrew pushed the throttles a little more, to reduce the roll. "We should punch out of this before we reach Safety Valve."

Visibility was nearly zero, and Andrew was steering the boat southward at ten knots, primarily using the chart plotter. Unable to get up on top of the water at that speed, the *Revenge* wallowed between the big, wind-driven rollers. The poor visibility prevented him from going any faster.

It took several minutes, but finally the downpour began to subside and then suddenly stopped altogether. They'd traveled nearly two miles since the last time they'd seen the trawler. Andrew had a good idea where Carmichael was going, though the radar currently showed the part of the bay where they'd last seen them was completely enveloped in the heavy rain they'd just come out of.

"Look here, Deuce," Andrew said, pointing to a spot on the chart plotter, just a little farther south. "Just this side of Soldier Key, see this shallow pass? The chart plotter shows five feet mean low water through the first part, but deepens after just a few yards. Remember Carmichael had insisted on riding through on a high tide, and he mentioned Soldier Key?"

"High tide will only give them a couple more feet," Deuce replied. "Jesse said the boat drafted nearly six. That would be fine if seas were calm. Carmichael's boat'll bounce the bottom in this chop."

Deuce scrolled the device northward. "Here. About a hundred yards north of Soldier Key. This would be my choice on a day like this. Ten feet of water at low tide all the way through the shoal."

Tony came around behind the two men at the helm. "That's got to be the one," he said. "It's got some turns and Carmichael said he'd need guides to get through the channel."

"Head south," Deuce said. "We'll wait a mile north of Soldier Key. They're lost in rain clutter, but when they come out of it, we'd see them a lot better from down there."

Andrew pushed the throttles forward, bringing the big boat up out of the water, as he glanced at the radar. The rain band Carmichael's boat was lost in wasn't far away, but they needed to move farther away, and the other boat would be near the edge of the radar's reliable range.

In another five minutes, Andrew brought the *Revenge* down off plane. The sun was shining, but to the east it looked like another line of storms was building.

"Where'd they go?" Deuce said, adjusting the radar's gain to maximum, as the rain squall the trawler had been lost in finally moved ashore. "They were right there just five minutes ago, two miles inshore from Stiltsville."

"We haven't heard anything on Jesse's listening device," Julie said. "Not since Carmichael started shouting orders when the rain was about to hit them."

"Head back to the channel," Deuce said. "Are those bugs waterproof?"

"No," Paul replied. "Think it just got wet? I'll activate the second one; this one's near the end of its power, anyway."

Andrew pushed the throttles to the stops, making a sweeping turn to the north. "Carmichael must have changed his mind," Andrew said. "If they're in Biscayne Channel, sea clutter from the breaking waves on the shoal could be hiding them on radar."

CHAPTER NINETEEN

"That doesn't look good," Charity said, leaning over to whisper to Chyrel, and pointing toward the dark clouds approaching the bay from the east.

Another storm had crossed the southern part of the bay earlier, and dark-gray sheets of rain were now slowly undulating across the Everglades.

Chyrel looked up at the fly bridge. Jesse's and Carmichael's heads were all that was visible over the low windshield. "They don't look concerned."

"Carmichael might not be," Charity whispered, "but Jesse is. That storm's going to catch us in just a few minutes.

A low scudding cloud passed over, darkening the sky. They'd watched as Jesse's boat turned and went out to sea minutes before. It was barely visible against the gray sky to the east. Then, suddenly, it was enveloped by the gray and was gone.

Sensing the changing barometer and feeling the charge in the air, Charity stood up. "I think we need to take cover," she said, just as a bolt of lightning struck the water to the east of a line of fishing cabins built over the water.

"We can't yet," Cruz replied, but jumped as the crack of thunder reached them. "Wilson wants us to stay up here until we reach the ocean."

Suddenly, the clouds seemed to burst open and rain started falling in sheets. Penny jumped up, squealing, and ran down the side deck for the shelter of the cabin. Jenna was right behind her, as Chyrel moved quickly down the other side of the boat. Cruz had no choice but to follow the two younger women.

The rain wasn't a concern for Charity. She'd spent more than one sleepless night at the helm during a storm.

"Get the girls inside!" Carmichael yelled down from the bridge. "Secure everything, and let me know when you have the wheel."

Once inside the salon, her hair plastered to her scalp by the rain, Charity turned and asked Cruz where they kept the towels.

Lifting the top of the navigation desk next to the door, Cruz pulled out a revolver and pointed it at them. "Move! Get your sweet asses down to the VIP cabin."

The two younger women screamed, as Charity froze in place for an instant. She knew that she could move quickly enough that the first shot would only injure her. She also knew that Cruz would never get a second shot off. But Chyrel and the two girls were behind her and they could be injured.

"Move!" Cruz screamed, thumbing the hammer back.

One by one, the women obediently went down the steps and into the cabin below the pilothouse. Once they were inside, Cruz closed the door. Charity heard a clicking sound and knew they'd been locked in.

"What's going on?" Penny asked, on the verge of tears.

"Why are you doing this?" Jenna yelled, pounding on the door.

"Shut up down there," Cruz shouted back, her voice muffled and coming from above. "Sit tight and get comfortable."

Looking up, Charity saw a trap door, with a ladder leading up to it. Usually roof hatches on boats had dogs, latches, or some other mechanism on the inside, to allow them to be opened. This one didn't.

"Shh," she whispered, holding a finger to her lips. Slowly, she stepped up on the first rung of the ladder, tilting her head to put an ear to the hatch. She could hear Cruz talking, either on a phone or intercom, telling Carmichael that she had the wheel.

Hearing scrambling noises from above, Charity pushed gently against the hatch. It didn't budge. From the stern, she could hear a scuffle taking place, then a loud thud, as if something had been dropped on the deck. She hoped it was Carmichael's body.

"What's going on?" Jenna wailed.

"Be quiet," Chyrel whispered softly. "We won't let anything happen to you." Then, eyeing the suitcases and Jesse's backpack on the bed, she touched Charity's shoulder. "Jesse's bag."

"Check it out," Charity said. "He's notorious for never going out on the water unarmed."

Opening the zipper, Chyrel saw nothing but clothes. She felt around, and pulled some out. "Nothing but clean shorts and tee-shirts."

"I saw Jesse offer Carmichael a cigar," Charity said, climbing down, and going to the drawers under the bed. "They were smoking them on the bridge."

Yanking open the first drawer and seeing nothing, she slammed it shut, then pulled open the one below it. Chyrel started on the other side.

When Charity opened the top middle drawer, her breath caught in her throat. "Thank you, oh wise and paranoid Jesse."

"Cigars?" Chyrel asked. "Was he planning to smoke them out?"

Lifting the box out, Charity felt it was heavier than it should be. "He was a sniper," she said, grinning, and opening the box. "Trained to hide in plain sight."

Pulling out two fistfuls of cigars, she set them aside then tilted the box to scoop out the remaining few. A small tag in the bottom read, *Made in the Dominican Republic*, and appeared to be sewn into the bottom of the lining. Tugging it slightly, she felt the bottom give and she lifted it out, removing Jesse's Sig Sauer P226 from where it was nestled on a soft foam pad that fit the box. Pulling the slide back slightly, she saw that he'd already chambered a round. Knowing Jesse, it was on top of a full magazine, but she slipped the magazine out and checked to make sure.

"Now it's eleven against six," Charity said, barely audible, as she slid the magazine back in with a click. "Bring it, bitch."

Above, Charity heard heavy footsteps, going up to the pilothouse.

"I dropped a pin on my handheld," she heard Carmichael say, his deeper voice resonating through the overhead. She assumed he meant that he'd marked a spot on the boat's GPS. "We'll come back and get what's left after the storm. I know the perfect place to ride it out for an hour or so."

The sound of the waves hitting the hull changed, and Charity sensed that they were turning. She thrust the handgun into the cargo pocket of her shorts and scrambled up onto the huge bed, moving to the single porthole.

Directly above her head, rain was pounding on the side deck. Water splashed against the porthole, and outside, visibility was only a few hundred feet. The boat was turning toward the shoal. She saw one of the stilt houses off the port bow, barely visible through the pouring rain. She continued to watch the water for a moment; the house disappeared forward of the boat as it turned.

"I think he's going to one of those houses built over the shoal," she said, scooting to the edge of the giant bed, and dropping down.

"Who are you?" Penny asked, moving warily away from the ladder.

Charity thought about it for a moment, before replying in a low voice, "We used to work for the government, but now we're freelancers. Wilson and Rosana? They're not who you think. They rape and torture women, before killing them. Right now, Ginger and I are the only thing standing between them and you."

"That can't be true," Jenna said. But there was no conviction in her voice.

"It is," Charity said firmly, pulling open the only other door in the cabin. A huge shower took up what was probably a full head at one time. "Get in here. If you hear shooting, don't come out until one of us tells you to."

"This can't be happening," Penny said, choking back tears. "We just wanted to party and have a good time."

"Everything's going to be okay," Chyrel said, quietly, putting a hand on the younger woman's shoulder and gently guiding her into the shower stall. "Let us do our jobs, okay? Then we'll get you home. Stretch is one of us, too."

"I didn't think he was like Wilson," Jenna muttered, following the blonde into the shower.

"He's not like anybody you ever met," Charity said, switching on a light inside the giant white room, and closing the door.

Chyrel turned to her partner and whispered, "Where's Jesse?"

"Unknown," Charity replied, her mind moving faster now as she surveyed the small cabin. She hefted the empty cigar box. It wasn't cheap cardboard. It was heavy, probably a hardwood. She handed it to Chyrel. "I need you up on the bed, as close to the wall as you can get. Have that box ready to bash the face of anyone who steps through the door."

Chyrel did as she was told and climbed up onto the bed. Kneeling on the edge with her back to the wall and left leg braced against the hull, she swung the cigar box like a tennis racket, judging her backhand distance to the door.

Charity looked around the cabin. The logical place for her would be crouched low, directly in front of the door and as far away from it as she could get. Unfortunately, that would put her in front of the shower. The only other choice was the far corner of the bed.

Climbing up onto it, she realized for the first time just how big the bed was. There was way more room than any two people would need, even three. In fact, with her back against the aft wall and the hull, Chyrel was a good ten feet away.

"Unless I'm hit," Charity began, looking right into her friend's eyes, "don't swing. You're my backup; I don't want you in my line of fire."

"Got it," Chyrel replied. Her expression was one of fear and awareness—a good combination, if tempered with reasoning.

The two women waited. Occasionally, a snippet of conversation could be heard from above. After a few minutes, Charity heard the pilothouse door closing, then feet moving toward the bow on the starboard side deck.

"It won't be long now," Charity whispered.

Chyrel nodded, flattening herself against the forward bulkhead as the sound of the engine dropped to an idle. The rocking motion decreased, and Charity knew they had entered water that was protected from the storm. A moment later, there was a scraping noise, as the boat bumped a dock or something, then the engine was shut off. Less light was coming through the porthole, and the inside of the cabin was dark.

Following the sound of footsteps with her eyes, Charity knew by the footfalls that it was Cruz moving aft to tie off to a dock at the house she had seen earlier. A moment later, Charity heard the aft salon door open and close. Above, she could just make out the two of them whispering.

Then nothing but silence.

Charity readied herself, knowing what was going to happen. The moment the door swung open, she planned to shoot whoever was on the other side. It was a conscious decision. She hadn't heard anything at all from Jesse and assumed he was either incapacitated or dead, but there was no time to think about him now.

Slowly, she thumbed the hammer back on the Sig. It had no safety, just a firing pin lock, and she knew that the only way to release that was to pull the trigger. A Sig Sauer handgun doesn't go off accidentally.

Suddenly, the door flew open, and Cruz was standing on the other side, pointing the short-barreled revolver straight into the cabin. In the microsecond it took for the woman to scan the room and see Charity, she didn't even have time to realize that it was the last thing she'd ever see.

Charity fired. At the same instant, she heard a sound from above. Time seemed to slow, as Charity realized her mistake and rolled forward on the bed, not even looking to see if Cruz were hit.

Carmichael must have realized that even with a gun, it was four to one, and his captives might be able to take Cruz down. Charity had figured that it might be the two of them coming through the door, but discounted it. The gun would be the advantage over a bunch of frightened women, and one or the other of them would probably be standing off to the side of the door.

She'd failed to take into account that they might use *both* entrances.

The report of a second round being fired inside the small cabin shocked her. Charity heard the shot ring out before she'd brought her gun up. Something tugged her hard into the mattress, and she saw Carmichael's face looking down at her through the open overhead hatch.

Slow-motion events unfolded in Charity's mind as the sound of Jesse's Sig striking the deck reached her ear. The clatter was drowned out by Chyrel's scream as Carmichael dropped through the opening, landing lightly on his feet.

Then the pain hit her.

CHAPTER TWENTY

C old saltwater hitting my face woke me instantly. Increased pressure on my ears told me I was underwater. I tried to reach in the direction I thought was up, but my hands were tied and heavy.

An anchor? I thought, thrashing around to get my hands loose.

My knee struck the sandy bottom and I rolled my legs under me, pushing off the seafloor with all my strength. Surprisingly, I instantly shot out of the water to my belly, even with the heavy anchor holding me down.

I gulped air, then was pulled back down again. Gathering my wits, I stood on the bottom, leaning into the strong current, and looked around as I tried to free my hands. But that wasn't going to happen until I could see what I was doing.

The water was about eight feet deep and clear, but I had no mask, so I could only make out vague shapes. The bottom seemed to rise to my right, so I pushed myself that way, letting the anchor help keep my upper body low against the flow of water. I planted my feet firmly with each side step, to keep from being sucked into the bay.

Squatting slightly, I pushed off the bottom again, timing it right this time. I exhaled hard, as I pulled the anchor up with me, and only my head broke the surface. I quickly grabbed a deep breath of air, before being pulled back under.

The back of my head hurt, but now it was clear and I knew that I was in my element, where patience is the over-riding prerequisite for survival. I've done free dives to a hundred feet, many times, holding my breath for more than a minute. One minute seems like a very short time, but a lot can be done in sixty seconds, if you take your time and don't waste energy struggling.

Slow is smooth, and smooth is fast, I reminded myself.

The body's urge to take a breath has a lot more to do with carbon dioxide buildup than lack of oxygen. Free diving required slow, deliberate movements to keep the diver's heart rate down. Decreasing the blood flow in an almost Zen-like manner used less oxygen and created less carbon dioxide. I began to slowly release a stream of bubbles from my lips, satisfying at least partially my body's need to exhale.

Trudging deliberately uphill toward a dark shape, I concentrated on my balance, holding the anchor in my hands, arms outstretched and limp, using no more muscle energy than my legs needed. I had to repeat the surfacing procedure three times. Each time I did, I lost several feet for every ten I gained trudging across the bottom.

Finally, I made it to a low coquina ledge, which barely reached mid-thigh. The surge told me I was close to the surface. I swung the heavy anchor to my right and it landed on top of the ledge. Without its weight, the current nearly pulled my feet out from under me. I pushed off the bottom and let the current lift me onto the ledge, as the anchor held me fast. The rough broken shells, loosely cemented together with limestone, cut into my knees. Ignoring the pain, I managed to get my feet under me and stood up.

The water was chest-deep, but a wave was bearing down on me. I had only a second to check my surroundings, before I had to drop low, to keep from being swept off the coquina ledge.

Just before I squatted under the wave, I glimpsed a large chunk of the same kind of sedimentary rock off to my right. Sandbars extended toward deep water just below the surface on either side of it.

As the wave rolled over me, I took advantage of the relatively calm water between waves and gathered the anchor in my hands, pushing off the top of the coquina ledge in an arcing dive into the swift moving current.

Again, I used the anchor to help balance my body, leaning into the flow, and sidestepped my way across the small natural channel. I only had to surface twice before I managed to bull my way onto the sandbar on the leeward side of the big rock. Both the rock and sandbar were submerged, but the rock created a breakwater from the waves. When I reached shallow water, I dropped to my knees, gulping air.

Waves broke over and around the rock, sending spray high over my head, before reforming in deeper water in the bay. After a moment, I was able to stand, the water only reaching my thighs.

Using my teeth, I got the knots loose and freed my hands. I'd been so busy just trying to stay alive, I hadn't noticed the storm raging all around me. Lightning flashed across the sky and the wind was driving the rain and salt spray nearly horizontal, when it gusted. The crashing of thunder was constant. I was standing on a small sandbar, a mile from any land, in the middle of a raging thunderstorm.

The anchor had a good ten feet of line attached to a short piece of chain. Not the sort of anchor one would use on Carmichael's big trawler. The chain had been wrapped around the anchor's flukes and was lashed in place with the braided rope, to ensure that there wasn't enough play to allow me to surface.

Then I remembered. The anchor had been lying in the bottom of the dinghy Carmichael had told me to check on. I hadn't been expecting him to try so soon, but he'd clubbed me with something. Gingerly, I touched the back of my head and winced. My hand came away bloody. I was soaked from the rain and seawater, so there was no way to tell how bad the bleeding was. But I knew scalp wounds bled profusely.

I peeled off my polo shirt, gently pulling it over my head. Taking a sleeve in one hand, and the tail from the opposite side in the other, I twirled it into a long bandage, and tied it tightly around my head. The pain sent flashes of electricity searing through my brain, and I dropped to one knee.

Finally, the pain subsided and I stood. We'd been about half a mile from reaching Biscayne Channel when the rain had hit and Carmichael jumped me. Looking south, I could just make out some of the stilt houses built along both banks of the channel. Others had been built farther to the south, but those were mostly destroyed over the years by either neglect or storms.

I was a quarter mile from the nearest of the houses that make up Stiltsville. Looking north, I could see the flash from the lighthouse, but couldn't make anything else out. That way, it was almost a mile to land.

We'd left the dock at noon, and the sun was now low in the western sky. I didn't relish the idea of being stuck on a sandbar at night. The house was the better choice.

High tide would come soon, and with it a short slack period where the current would be calm even if the sea wasn't. After that, it would change direction, pulling water out of the bay. I'd have to wait until slack tide, or risk being caught up in the current. And I'd have to swim the quarter mile before the flow changed and sucked me out to sea.

Although the lightning and thunder was almost constant, I heard the distinct sound of two gunshots, too close together to be a single gun. I knew it for what it was instantly and crouched behind the huge outcropping of coquina, getting low in the water.

The gunshots came from a distance. Sound travels better over water, even in a rainstorm. The shots came from beyond the stilt houses standing along the sides of the channel. I needed to get to one of those houses fast, and hope someone was there, or that there was a radio I could use to call for help.

The waves were still big but had begun to decrease in size since the heart of the storm had washed over the bay. Discounting the surge from the waves, I could tell the current was beginning to lessen. Just as I was about to dive in and swim to the nearest stilt house, I heard the sound of twin diesel engines approaching.

Out of the mist, I saw my boat heading into the channel from offshore. It slowed at the outer markers for a moment, then I saw the bow rise, as the *Revenge* accelerated up on plane and into the channel.

Standing and waving wildly with both arms over my head, I tried to signal one of the men on the boat. But the *Revenge* continued past the last of the stilt houses and turned south in the bay.

"Dammit," I yelled.

Half a mile south of me, the *Revenge* slowed again, then suddenly turned and came back toward me. It was obvious they were searching for Carmichael's boat. I stepped away from the rock and the surf splashing around and over it, and moved west, toward the open bay, again waving both arms over my head.

The red and green navigation lights on the bow flashed on and off twice. They'd seen me.

Diving headlong into the water, I began to swim out to deeper water as the *Revenge* slowed and settled into the chop just a hundred feet away. A few minutes later, Tony reached down and helped me onto the swim platform.

"What happened?" he asked. "We lost the trawler in the storm. Did it sink?"

"Carmichael surprised me," I said, loud enough for Deuce to hear on the bridge. I opened a small cabinet, and dried myself with one of the towels I keep there. "Tossed me overboard with an anchor tied to my wrists."

Finn was going nuts in the salon, so I opened the door. He nearly knocked my legs from under me, bowling sideways into my knees and sitting on my feet, his great tail thumping the deck. I bent down and gave him a belly rub, telling him to stay in the cockpit.

Tony and I climbed quickly to the bridge. "Any sign of them?" I asked, as Andrew rose and moved over to the bench seat.

"We lost them completely on radar," Deuce said. "Did he give you any idea where he was headed?"

"No," I replied, studying the radar. The seven fixed echoes from the remaining houses were clearly visible, as well as the four towers marking the entrances to Biscayne Channel, though none but the nearest were visible through the light rain. The echo from a fifth tower wasn't visible on the screen, due to rain scatter. It was nearly a mile to the south, marking the shallow entrance to a deeper, natural channel that was rarely used.

"All he ever said was Soldier Key," I said, looking all around. "There's no way that Carmichael's boat could get more than a couple of miles from here."

"Where?" Deuce asked, touching a finger to his ear and studying the radar image.

Realizing that he was listening to someone on his comm, I opened a cabinet in the overhead and grabbed one of the spare earwigs we'd put there.

I switched it on, stuck it in my ear, and said, "Repeat your last."

"Thank God you're safe," I heard Julie say. "We found their boat using the infrared setting on the rooftop camera."

The closed-circuit TV monitor switched to infrared, clearly showing a bright hot spot about a mile to the south.

"Zoom in," I said, leaning closer.

As the image became larger the one big hot spot seemed to grow tentacles out of the top. They moved back and forth across the large white spot, which I recognized as the heat signature from a boat's engines. Suddenly, the tentacles moved away from the big white spot and it became clear that it was five people, walking on a pier.

"There should be six," Deuce said.

"That's gotta be them," I said. "Tied up close to one of the houses, so the boat looked like part of the house on radar." I turned and faced Deuce. "Just before you guys came through the channel, I heard two gunshots."

Deuce looked out over the water. The nearer houses were barely visible, but the ones down on the shallower channel were still shrouded in misty rain.

"The sky's clearing," Deuce said. "There's no way we can get anywhere near there, without being seen."

"Not on *top* of the water," Tony interjected.

"Break out the scooters, Tony," I said. "Andrew, grab two sets of rebreather equipment from under the aft couch in the salon."

"You're not going," Deuce said. "That shirt wrapped around your head is soaked with blood."

"I'm going," Andrew said, his voice determined and menacing, as he moved toward the ladder.

"You and Tony," I said, sitting down at the helm. "You'll need to hurry. It'll be dark in an hour."

The sun was nearly touching the distant treetops on the far side of the bay when Tony stepped off the swim platform. Reluctantly, I'd moved the *Revenge* away from the house, further into the bay to the northwest.

Stiltsville was fully inside Biscayne National Park, and Carmichael might find a fishing boat inside the park boundaries suspicious. And we didn't want him to see divers with underwater scooters getting into the water.

Andrew and Deuce moved the scooters through the transom door, handing one down to Tony in the water.

Deuce had rigged two dock lines from the bow; Tony quickly swam the scooter to the starboard side, away from the house, and attached it to one of the lines.

"Be careful," Deuce said, "but do what you have to do to get Charity and Chyrel back."

Andrew nodded somberly then slipped quietly into the water. Deuce handed the other scooter down to him, and Andrew swam it around to join Tony.

When they were ready, with Deuce standing by the rail just above them, I engaged the transmissions and started idling to the south. This was a dangerous way to make an insertion. If either diver let go of their scooter, they might be sucked under by the boat's huge propellers.

Deuce signaled me to increase speed, and I bumped the throttles up slightly. Night had fallen and the storm had passed, but the waves out on the ocean were still too big for a slow-moving trawler. It appeared as if Carmichael was staying put until morning.

Passing the last of the stilt houses, still half a mile away in the bay, I saw the trawler tied up to one of the docks. The engines were cooling, giving them more definition on the IR feed. This house had a long pier out to deep water on the south side, and a smaller one with finger docks for bay boats, to the north. Carmichael was tied up close to the house itself.

When we were parallel to the shallower channel, I shifted the engines to neutral for a moment, as Deuce untied the lines, freeing the two divers.

A moment later, Andrew's voice came over the comm. "We're clear." Both he and Tony were wearing full-face scuba masks, which enabled them to talk.

Checking the compass and radar, I said, "Make your heading zero-nine-five degrees, Andrew. Range is about eight-hundred yards."

"Roger that."

Tony and Andrew were both accomplished divers; it sort of goes with the territory of being a Navy SEAL and Coast Guard Maritime Enforcement. Each scooter was equipped with a compass and knot meter. All they had to do was calculate how long it would take to cover the distance at whatever speed the scooters would go. The streamlined rebreathers didn't have the added drag of a scuba tank, so they could probably cover the half-mile in six or seven minutes.

"I don't know how we could have missed it," Deuce said, climbing up to the bridge as I engaged the transmissions again.

"Rain blocked the radar," I said. "And breaking waves prevented you seeing them from offshore, even with the camera."

Studying the infrared image on the monitor, I could tell there were people inside the house. Body heat doesn't take long to change the surface temperature of windows, which are usually cooler than the walls of an unoccupied building because they allow light to go through, where the walls absorb it. The windows were noticeably warmer than the walls.

We idled south for about half a mile, then turned around. It wasn't uncommon for night fishermen to go back and forth over known hot spots, trolling bait behind the boat.

When I started the second turn, Andrew's voice came over the comm again. "We're at the boat. Tony's going aboard to check it out."

The minutes turned into hours as Deuce and I waited on the bridge, watching the house slip by again.

"He's not going anywhere." Andrew's voice seemed to boom in my ear. "Keel's buried several inches into the sand already."

"There's a body in the forward cabin," Tony whispered. "It's Cruz, shot once in the face."

A moment later, Tony said, "Blood on the bed in the lower cabin. Nobody else on board."

"One of the others must be injured," I said. "The hatch to that cabin can be locked from the outside. They must have herded the women in there, after he clobbered me. Do you see a cigar box?"

"Yeah, cigars are laying all over the place," Tony whispered.

"Any sign of my gun?" I asked. "It was in the cigar box."

"You mean besides the hole in Cruz's face?" Tony replied. "Brass on the bed, a single nine-millimeter casing."

"Charity shot Cruz," I mumbled.

"There's a bullet hole in the mattress," Tony said. "Near vertical entry."

"Get back in the water," Deuce ordered. "See if there's a way inside without walking that long pier."

Turning around once more, we moved slowly toward the house again. Then Tony's voice came over the comm. "There's a ladder mounted on one of the stilts."

The minutes ticked past slowly. I knew what they were doing. If the ladder led to the deck around the house, or to a trap door inside, they'd have to remove their gear to get up it. They each had the dock lines from the scooters, so they could tie it and their gear to one of the pilings.

"Going covert," Tony said. The two men were probably underwater, taking one last breath before ascending the ladder. From there, they'd limit any talking.

Turning the wheel, I aimed the bow of the *Revenge* toward the shallow channel. Carmichael's boat probably cleared the sand bar at the western approach to the house by inches. The *Revenge* would have a couple of feet. Using the forward-scanning sonar, I followed the deeper water toward the house. If Carmichael saw us now, all the better.

Tony's voice was barely audible. "Trap door to the inside of the house. Not locked. Can you give us a diversion?"

"Hit the spotlight," I told Deuce.

Reaching up, Deuce turned the handle of the roof mounted spotlight, aiming it directly at the house. When he switched it on, the whole house was caught in the powerful beam. We could clearly see Tony and Andrew hanging on a ladder just below the middle of the house.

Over the comm, we heard Tony and Andrew slam the trap door open, climbing quickly and shouting. A single shot rang out.

"What's going on?" Deuce asked, leaning on the rail.

"Carmichael's down," Andrew said. "Still breathing, but I can fix that. Charity's been shot, but seems okay."

"Tie him up," Deuce said. "We'll be at the dock for extraction in just a minute."

The bottom fell away to deeper water in the natural channel that ran past the house. I bumped the throttles up and maneuvered toward it as Deuce quickly climbed down the ladder. Over the comm, I heard Andrew asking each woman if she was okay.

I kept the light on the house as Deuce jumped onto the dock with both the bow and stern lines in hand. Once the boat was secure, we both raced toward the house. The door opened, and Tony stepped out, grinning.

"Chyrel has a cool idea," he said, leading the two younger women out of the house.

Chyrel helped Charity out onto the deck as Deuce and I approached. Charity's upper arm was wrapped tightly with gauze, but a spot of blood seeped through.

"How bad?" I asked Charity when she looked up at me.

"I won't be playing tennis for a while," she replied. "The bullet went through, but I don't think it hit the bone."

"Get her aboard," Deuce told Chyrel, and turned to the two younger women. "Are you two all right?"

"Who are you people?" Jenna asked.

"The less you know right now, the better," I said. "For now, just rest assured that you're safe. We'll make sure you get home that way."

"Go with Tony," Deuce said, then disappeared through the door.

The two girls followed the others and I went inside the house. Andrew was standing over Carmichael, whose eyes went wide when he saw me.

"Will he live?" Deuce asked Andrew.

"He'll survive the gunshot wound," Andrew replied. "Or was that a rhetorical question?"

"Don't kill him," Chyrel's voice said over my earwig. "I have a better idea."

"Who the hell are you, Stretch?" Carmichael asked. "If you're a cop or something, I got rights."

"You have the right to shut the fuck up," Andrew growled, his voice low and uncharacteristically menacing. "If you give up that right and say another word, I'll break your scrawny neck."

"Just give me a few minutes, big guy," Chyrel said. "We almost got it." When she returned, she placed a sheet of paper on a table, and handed Andrew a length of boat line. "Tie him up so he won't get loose," she said.

"What's your idea?" Deuce asked.

Chyrel grinned and held up what I recognized as a small computer flash drive. "Everything we dug up on the two of them is saved on this."

I picked up the sheet of paper and read the computer-printed note.

This guy is wanted by the United States Army in connection with multiple unsolved murder cases.

It was late before we got back to the hotel. We'd waited until we were in the middle of the bay before Chyrel called 911 and reported someone trespassing in one of the stilt houses. She'd also told the dispatcher that she'd heard gunshots.

Then she tossed her cellphone in the water.

"I'm flying back tonight," I told Andrew, after we'd packed everything up in the room and were ready to leave. "You and Tony can rest up on the boat and head back in the morning."

"I'm going with you," Charity said. "I don't like being away from the boat for so long."

Chyrel had rechecked and rebandaged Charity's wound. The bullet had gone through the meaty part of her upper arm, leaving a slightly larger exit wound. Both would heal, but it would take time. She didn't need any stitches, and she refused any kind of medication. We said our good-byes to the others, then drove to the airport, taking Finn along. He didn't like flying, but I didn't want to be away from him any longer.

Less than an hour later, we were winging over Florida Bay, heading back to my island and normalcy. Landing on the water at night was a little trickier than in daylight, but the shallow water of the flats north of my island was smooth and calm, with a bright moon overhead. As I circled around, I noticed a light on in my little house. I was certain I'd turned everything off before leaving, but maybe Tony or Andrew had left a light on.

Once we were down, I left the landing lights on and approached the end of the floating dock. Charity stepped out onto the pontoon, ready to fend us away if need be.

Suddenly, a figure stepped out of the darkness at the foot of the pier. It was Devon.

"What are you doing here?" I asked, after shutting the engine down and climbing out of the *Hopper*. Finn raced down the pier and disappeared around the west bunkhouse. I had my backpack, and a small chest under my arm. "I thought you had to work tonight."

"We finished early," she replied, clearly shaken up about something.

"What's wrong?"

"Jesse, your boat is gone."

"It's okay," I said, hugging her tightly. "Andrew and Tony have it. They'll be back tomorrow"

"That's a relief. Did you finish what you were doing in Miami?"

Charity smiled. "I'd say it's being wrapped up right about now."

Devon looked at each of us in turn. "You made the recovery and turned the perps over to law enforcement?"

"Something like that," I said. "At any rate, yeah, we got Amy Huggins's property back, and the people who stole it won't bother anyone again."

"I want to hear all about it," she said. Then she noticed the bandage around Charity's arm. "You got hurt?"

"Flesh wound," Charity said. "Nothing to bother a doctor about."

"You two are probably exhausted," Devon said. "Let me fix something to eat."

"I could eat," I replied, uncoiling the water hose. "Y'all go ahead, I just need a few minutes to wash down the *Hopper*, get some of the salt spray off the old girl."

"The only difference between men and boys—" Devon began.

Charity finished the sentence as the two women walked toward the foot of the pier: "—is the price of their toys."

EPILOGUE

F riday morning, Deuce called before we were even out of bed. I groggily pulled on a pair of shorts and got to my feet, then tiptoed into the living room.

"Have you seen the news this morning?" he asked.

"I just woke up," I replied quietly.

"The Coast Guard, responding to an anonymous tip last night, arrested former Staff Sergeant Wilson Carmichael on suspicion of murder."

"I guess they found the flash drive?"

"All they're saying on the news is that Carmichael was an escaped federal prisoner and that Army CID was en route to Miami to take him back into custody."

I knew that Chyrel had probably found out more. "What are they not saying on the news?"

"The CID agent that's coming to take him back to Leavenworth is the same guy who was investigating the murder of Captain Huggins and his men."

Looking out the big, south-facing window, I noticed that Charity's boat was gone. I quickly told Deuce I had to go, then went out onto the deck and around the corner. From the southeast corner of the deck, I could see the length of Harbor Channel. The air was crisp and cool, visibility unlimited.

And Charity's boat was nowhere to be seen.

How did she start the engine and leave without me hearing it? I wondered.

Then I noticed that the wind had changed. The cooler air was the result of a northerly breeze. She'd simply loosed the lines, raised the foresail, and sailed away from the dock. I went back inside, feeling as if something was now missing.

On the table was a sheet of paper. I picked it up and read it.

Jesse,

Sorry for leaving without saying goodbye. I'm not very good with that. When I woke up, the wind was right and every fiber of my being wanted to sail away. The bullet hole notwithstanding, I had a great time with you and Devon last night. It was nice to see everyone else again, as well. Tell them all I said goodbye, will you? And if you ever need me, I still have the phone.

Charity

Throughout the day, I picked up bits and pieces on the news about what had happened in Stiltsville. Tony and Andrew did a thorough job of wiping everything down that the women might have touched, so I felt confident nothing would lead back to us.

When we arrived at the marina, I offered the two younger women a ride to anywhere they wanted to go.

They thanked me, and Jenna said that a friend lived just a block away, and called her for a ride.

Over the weekend, I made a few calls to friends, who called in a few more friends. I also called all the building supply places in the Middle Keys until I found the one that Amy Huggins was buying material from. I told them to deliver everything she had on order first thing Monday morning, and that I'd pay for it on delivery.

On Sunday, I took Devon back to the *Anchor* and then stopped at No Name Key on the way back to the island. When I knocked on the trailer door it opened immediately. Amy saw the little chest under my arm, and her eyes welled up with tears.

"You got it back?"

"Minus about a dozen stones," I replied. "But more than enough to finish your house and set you up for the rest of your life."

She invited me in and I placed the little chest on the table in the dining room. When I lifted the lid, Amy's mouth fell open.

"Four hundred and eighty-two stones, including the one you loaned me. Each one identical in size and shape, and worth about five grand each."

Amy staggered slightly and I quickly caught her hand and led her to a chair. "That's almost a quarter of a million dollars," she said, her voice quaking.

"You missed a zero," I said.

She looked up at me in utter disbelief. "You mean—"

"Two-point-five million," I said, sitting down next to her. "But there's a catch."

"What do you mean?"

"Each stone could be sold individually to any number of people for twice that amount. But you can't flood the market with them; they're too recognizable."

"They're stolen, then," she said, her mouth turning downward.

"Many times," I replied. "The rightful owner has been dead for centuries and there's no way to trace any heir. Your husband came by them honestly, but more than one government would like to take them from you."

"So how can I turn them into cash?"

"I know someone," I said. "He knows the right people for this, and says he can turn them into a million in cash in less than a week."

"A million dollars?" Amy asked, picking up one of the stones and looking at it.

"Or, you can go through this same guy and sell them off one at a time over the next several years for twice that. Maybe more."

"Here," she said, picking up three more stones and thrusting them toward me. "These are for you."

"No, Amy," I said. "I told you what my price was. A cold beer at the *Rusty Anchor*, and you donate a little something to the Watermen Foundation. Just tell Pam Lamarre at the bank, and she'll handle everything. Completely anonymous."

She started to struggle to her feet and I helped her up. She looked as though she was going to give birth any minute. Throwing her arms around my neck, she blubbered into my shoulder for a moment. I held her until it passed.

She stepped back, wiping tears from her eyes. "How can I ever repay you for this?"

"Raise your son to know who and what his father was, Amy," I said, taking her by the shoulders. "He wasn't just an Army officer."

I went on to tell her all the things about her husband's service that she didn't know anything about. I told her about a new star that now hung on the wall at Langley, and though there was no name attached to it, those who knew, knew, and were very grateful for his service. We talked until it was nearly dark. She agreed that I'd take the emeralds down to Key West for her, to let Buck Reilly find a new home for them.

"In the meantime," I said. "You have a house to finish. I took the liberty of setting up a delivery tomorrow morning. Everything you had on your order. I'll take the cost of that out of what we get from Buck."

"There's no way I can arrange workers today," she said.

"Took care of that, too. I doubt any will be licensed contractors, but they'll be here in the morning along with the material."

The next morning, the work crew numbered sixteen, and more arrived after lunch. Over the next several days, we worked hard from before sunrise to well past sunset, stopping only to eat and watch the sun go down. The house quickly started looking like a home.

Buck came through, as promised, delivering one-point-two million in cash the following Friday. The exterior of the house had already been finished, and in five days' time all we had left to do was to set the cabinets and fixtures. It was a quaint little Conch house, and Dan Huggins, Junior was born in it a week after we moved the furniture in.

By November, I still hadn't heard anything from Charity. Kim came down to celebrate the Marine Corps birthday with us at the *Anchor* and asked if I'd read the recent review on our website.

"It's kind of weird, Dad," she said. "And I don't see any charter that you took the person out on. I mean, it was scheduled, but you didn't even enter the fishing report afterword."

"What did it say?" I asked.

Kim took her phone out, tapped the screen a few times, and turned it so I could read it. The review was from two days ago.

Outstanding adventure. I found our butterflies and two nasty bottom-dwellers. The crew made me feel at home like I hadn't felt in a long time. The captain and his mate took great care in seeing to it that I was pleased. Will definitely book them again.

About a week later, on a beautiful Tuesday evening in late November, I dropped the hook half a mile off Middle Cape Sable. I wasn't sure why I'd come all the way across Florida Bay to one of the most remote beaches in the state, or anywhere else for that matter, but I just felt the urge to be somewhere else.

The nearest civilization was miles away and the beach was accessible only by boat. I was anchored in eight feet of water and had a line out, but wasn't really expecting anything. I'd just wanted to get away for a day.

A light breeze was coming off the cape, pointing the stern straight toward a cloudless sunset. Gulls squawked and laughed on the beach, but I was far enough away that they were barely audible. Other than that, the only other sound was the gentle, rhythmic lapping of water around the hull.

The sun was nearing the horizon, and I'd already decided to just stay here for the night. I was far enough from shore that the mosquitoes wouldn't be able to sense my body heat—though they were few and far between up here in late November anyway. Since it was a weekday, there wasn't another boat in sight.

I was alone on the sea—just me, Finn, the *Revenge*, and the beach. All around, it was quiet and serene. Hearing a whooshing sound, I looked toward the direction it came from. A swirling in the water showed me where the dolphin had surfaced. A moment later it surfaced again, fifty yards away.

The serenity was shattered by the loud chirping sound up on the bridge. The satellite phone. The one that only had a single phone number programmed into it.

Climbing quickly to the bridge, I grabbed it, and punched the *Accept* button. "Charity?"

"Hi, Jesse," she said, a whimsical sigh in her voice.

"Where are you?" I asked, as I sat in the captain's chair. Opening the little fridge, I took out a cold Red Stripe and opened it, spinning the chair around and putting my feet up on the aft rail.

"Little Cayman," she said. "I'm back on my own boat now. What are you doing? Busy?"

"Feet up, anchor down," I replied. "I'm watching the sunset from the bridge, anchored off Cape Sable with an ice cold adult beverage."

There was silence for a moment. Then she said, "Where that whole mess started a couple of years ago."

Charity was referring to a man and woman that had been murdered just down the beach on East Cape. It was one event in many that were meant to draw me out, so a Haitian drug gang in Miami could get their hands on me. Charity had disappeared during the search, when the gang had gassed my island, knocking everyone out and they'd hauled me up to the Ten Thousand Islands.

"Bad things happen everywhere. It's not the fault of the location."

Another long pause. She had something on her mind, otherwise she wouldn't have called.

"Sorry for leaving without saying goodbye," she finally said. In the background, I could hear boat sounds. She was on the water.

"Are you watching the sunset, too?" I asked, letting her get to her question in her own way.

"Every evening," she replied. Then there was another pause. "I just called to say thank you."

"For what?" I asked.

"For just being you," she said. "For listening, even when I wasn't saying anything. It meant a lot. And a big thanks for helping me find out about my boat."

"Glad to be of help," I said, as the sun and sea began to merge in a dazzling display of color and dance.

Over the phone, I heard Charity's breath catch and realized that in degrees of longitude, we weren't very far apart and the light show I was witnessing on the Gulf was the same one she was seeing in *El Caribe*.

"You could have had me," she said, finally getting to the reason she'd called. "And you're an easy man to fall for."

"Two ships in the night," I said.

She laughed. "Part of me is going to miss the excitement," she said, as I watched the last of the sun disappear with a green flash of light.

THE END

If you'd like to receive my newsletter for specials, book recommendations, and updates on coming books, please sign up on my website:

WWW.WAYNESTINNETT.COM

THE CHARITY STYLES CARIBBEAN THRILLER SERIES
Merciless Charity
Ruthless Charity
Reckless Charity

THE JESSE MCDERMITT
CARIBBEAN ADVENTURE SERIES

Fallen Out
Fallen Palm
Fallen Hunter
Fallen Pride
Fallen Mangrove
Fallen King
Fallen Honor
Fallen Tide
Fallen Angel
Fallen Hero
Rising Storm

The Gaspar's Revenge Ship's Store is now open. There you can purchase all kinds of swag related to my books.
WWW.GASPARS-REVENGE.COM